DIARY
OF A
RETIREE

PAUL COATES

First Edition

ISBN 978-0-6455637-3-3

"Age is an issue of mind over matter. If you don't mind, it doesn't matter."

Mark Twain

"Old age isn't so bad if you consider the alternative."

Maurice Chevalier

"You are only young once, but you can stay immature indefinitely."

Ogden Nash

There are three signs that you are getting older. The first is memory loss … but I forget the other two.

Unattributed

TABLE OF CONTENTS

DAY ONE

I woke up at my usual hour even though, for the first time in my adult life, I no longer needed to jump up, moan about my lack of sleep, shower and go to work. Just as well, because I had no feeling in my legs. Bending my neck at an eye watering ninety degrees, I peered down to the foot of the bed and quickly identified the problem. Snoring gently, the fur covered source of my impeded blood circulation was laying on my feet. Hours of Alfie's body weight had done the trick. Propping myself up on my elbows, I was greeted by expectant brown eyes urging me to get up and take him on his morning walk. He is like a ninja dog, the slightest movement on the bed and he goes from deep slumber to demand mode.

I told Alfie that there was no rush. I was not under a time constraint for his walk because I no longer had to go to work. He responded with an unchanged expression and a tentative wag to encourage me to act.

I was free.

No work, no schedule of meetings, no one on ones, no interviews, no reports to write, no nothing. An empty diary. Nothing in the calendar, no-one wanting to see me. No dealing with the growing minority of entitled, needy staff who think their employers are responsible for solving the problems in their private life. No longer having to nod sympathetically and sign off another 'wellness' day for those who are too well to attend work. Nor having to listen to the Gen Y or Z who draw upon their two year's work experience to advise me on how I should run the organisation more successfully. One might think that my own hard-earned qualifications and forty-five years' work experience (fifty-five including childhood jobs from dishwashing to serving hotdogs) would at least render me worthy of one or two good ideas. Apparently not.

But perhaps I am just what they think I am, a dinosaur. Strange that these noble powerful beasts are used in the pejorative sense. I have to say that I think the dinosaurs get a bad rap and frankly it's a tad disrespectful. Occasionally I think of pointing out that dinosaurs survived for 165 million years on earth. If mankind continues to bugger up the planet, it is unlikely to survive one per cent of the dinosaurs' existence.

Where was I? Yes, freedom. I'm retired with buggerall things on my 'to do' list.

Alfie twists his head. A habit he has when trying to fully understand the human language. He does, of course, comprehend the situation and looks over to my bedside table drawing my attention to a handwritten note and giving me the "not so fast" expression.

I reach over and pick up the paper. Kerryn has left me her carefully crafted 'to do' list as opposed to the usual peck on the cheek before she breezed out of the bedroom dressed to sort out the world. She is an executive at a social housing organisation and I am officially a 'has-been.' Being a few years younger than me, thoughts of retirement are far from her mind. A cursory glance at the list quickly dispels any naive notion that I am retired. Looks like I've got a not-so-new boss and a brand-new job description.

I have added a line of my own to the 'to do' list.

I am going to write a daily diary (groans from the reader).

Now before you discard this book thinking to yourself '*Jesus, the diary of a retiree this is going to be as riveting as watching paint dry.*' STOP NOW. I can't promise you Mission Impossible or James Bond, but I can make certain guarantees. Within this book you will find pathos, humour, tales of 'derring do' (as they say in Victorian novels), legendary sporting moments, courtroom drama, fighting the systems and I may, or may not, throw in a couple of sizzling gypsies.

"Hang on a minute" … I hear the perceptive ones amongst you crying 'foul.' Sceptically, you ask how, if I am about to write a diary, can I make those promises, (unless you are one of those fortune telling gypsies mentioned above)? I can answer that question along with a minor confession. I did wonder about the content myself when I started, but having completed the diary and re-read it, I was able to add the above claims as an afterthought.

So, there's your guarantee, buckle in.

DAY FIVE

Okay, I have jumped to day five, so the diary won't have daily entries. Things got in the way, not least Kerryn's list which, incidentally, is still only one third complete. Well, what does she expect? I'm a busy man.

With a sceptical raise of her eyebrow the obvious enquiry follows. "Busy doing what?"

"'Things," I reply.

Alfie's on the balcony barking. He spends a lot of time on the balcony barking (we live on the upper floor of the house) and pretty much has the best view in the suburb overlooking the Indian ocean. This means there is a lot of activity around the place with walkers, scantily clad beach goers of all genders (and non-binaries), cyclists, scooter fiends, and cars, as well a steady flow of locals who live in the surrounding streets. Alfie does have a barking hit list.

Here is the hit list in order of priority.

Dogs who dare to walk down his street.

Owners of said dogs.

Strangers walking by who don't live in the street.

Unknown visitors to the house

Delivery people.

Now I could create a subcategory, but it is, be warned, slightly controversial. There is possibly, and I emphasise 'possibly,' a racist streak in Alfie. It may be my imagination, but his barking seems more vigorous if the dog, dog's owner, stranger, or delivery person is … black. I took him to the Vet to discuss the problem, but no professional opinion was forthcoming. Whilst they can point me in the direction of all sorts of training, including how to respond to snakes, they do not do cultural awareness training for canines. Which I have to say was disappointing.

Now category 5 above is interesting because we get a lot of these. Kerryn's appetite for online ordering is capacious, which means there is a constant flow of parcels being delivered. Twenty per cent of these deliveries fail at the last hurdle and are re-directed to the local post office.

Now I accept that it is a sad fact that two things continue to grow as we get older, these being cynicism and our ears. My ears are proportionately bigger; I'm looking more like a Hobbit every day. Driven by my ever-growing cynicism, I convinced myself that the delivery people were being less than diligent regarding their attempts at placing the ordered goods at the house of the intended recipient. In response, I devised a cunning plan to test the theory. Alfie was key to the success of my plan. Whilst he stood guard on the balcony, I waited below at our front door ready to pounce when he raised the alarm.

It, sort of, went to plan. Alfie started barking vigorously. So much so, I assumed the delivery driver must be close and waited for the knock on the door. No knock. So, after a few seconds I rushed out to catch the lazy culprit disappearing into the distance. He took the form of a young man and was climbing back into the cab of his lorry. He stared back in fright at the vision of an insane (big eared?) pensioner rushing towards him with a rabid dog raising hell on the balcony above. "Why didn't you knock," I shouted. "I'm bloody sick of getting cards telling me you tried to make a delivery, but no-one was home." More fist shaking followed by a final insult. "I've had a gutful of driving to your depot every bloody day. You're a lazy sod."

He slammed the van door shut and reversed out of the driveway shaking his head whilst holding the steering wheel with his right hand and pointing with his left. Perplexed, I looked in the direction at which he was pointing and saw a package nestled safely to the right of our front door. I turned to wave an apology but was too late. As the van sped off down the street, I looked up to the balcony and met the eyes of Alfie who just stared down at me in silence. He was done barking but pricked up his ears and twisted his head in a sort of canine equivalent of a shrug.

DAY EIGHT

The parcel debacle has come home to roost in the form of a short letter from the delivery company. I won't re-produce the whole letter, but here is the summary paragraph.

In conclusion Mr Coates, following the complaint by our delivery driver, Mr Kwame Mutunga, I am authorised to warn you that any further incidents of this nature will result in a permanent embargo of deliveries to your home address. Should this eventuate, you will be required to collect future deliveries from our depot in Balcatta.

Martin Savage

Head of Operations

I decided to keep the details of the incident to myself and destroyed the letter to avoid Kerryn's wrath. But there were several take-aways from the whole affair. Firstly, I didn't want to end up having to trek all the way to Balcatta every time Kerryn had ordered something online. I multiplied the number of orders she made per week by the number of kilometres to the Balcatta depot and estimated I would be on the road for an extra 2000 kilometres every year.

Aside from the fact that I also needed to check that parcels had been left by the front door before abusing the delivery person, there was one very interesting canine related learning. Alfie's barking was particularly vigorous during the incident which I believe heightened my own emotions. Not that I am justifying my behaviour by blaming Alfie but just giving context. What became clear to me was that there definitely is a racist element to Alfie's behaviour.

I can hear Alfie barking again, sounds like we have another delivery and judging by the volume it could be Mister Mutunga.

DAY NINE

Checked the post, no parcels today. Three items in the post box. A rates bill, a leaflet, and a Shit Kit. The latter being a periodic request to defecate into an unfeasibly small jar which I then post off to the other side of the country for some poor sod to open and test for bowel cancer. Oh! the joys of old age, I'd rather be a lab technician.

Annoying as they are, at least the Shit Kit senders are well meaning which is more than I can say for author of the leaflet. Local bloody Estate Agents are a pain in the arse and top of the list is a partnership by the name of 'Timewasters, Annoying and Pointless' (TAP for short, real name not used for legal reasons). You know the type, gelled hair, overly tight suits, pointy shoes, no socks, and a smile that wouldn't look out of place in a Crocodile's family album.

Setting my prejudices aside, I observed that TAP felt the need to tell me how well they are doing, at what they do, through the medium of a colourful glossy leaflet. Maybe some people are keen to learn that they, TAP that is, sold a couple of houses this week. I, for one, do not need a regular update of their performance and achievements in the workplace. Selling houses is their job, isn't it? I don't get a leaflet from the local carpenter updating me on the built-in wardrobes she has installed or the food delivery man recounting the number of tepid Meatlover pizzas he successfully dropped off to the wrong address. So why in God's name do TAP feel the need to do this. Insecurity? Arrogance?

Alfie's on the balcony barking at the appropriate passersby (refer day five above). The volume increased briefly so I presume their ethnicity cannot be categorised as Caucasian.

Not everyone fears Alfie. My immediate neighbours Erin and Bernie are lovely people and, being big fans of him, are unfazed by his vocalisations. Well, I guess he does have a charm, but then again so did Hitler. In contrast to Alfie's efforts, they offer a far more melodious contribution to the neighbourhood airwaves. Erin is a singer who keeps claiming she has retired. Today we have had an Andy Williams medley and one of my favourites, 'Music to watch girls by,' floats up the street. Even Alfie is now quiet, sitting attentively with his ears pricked.

DAY FIFTEEN

Yeah, I know, I missed a couple of diary days. But it's been bloody hot here. Forty degrees centigrade, aircon running at full tilt, as is Kerryn's whinging. She hates the heat. She's from Perth, we met in London, she wanted to come back here and now whinges. Go figure. Anyway, you don't need to know the ins and outs of my relationship dynamic.

Just picture blue cloudless skies, scantily clad young people walking along the ocean pathway and surfers on the waves (a popular surf spot called 'Toms' is just in front of us, and we get front seats from the balcony).

I don't get surfing. They bob around for hours rejecting waves which are apparently not good enough (if you're too cool for school that is). Eventually, when a wave is deemed worthy, they ride it. I say ride it if you can call moving forward for five seconds, a ride. Problem is that the latter one's are few and far between. A lot of waiting for little tangible benefit. A bit like going to the GP.

But I digress. If you've got the picture that it's not a day for a man in his mid-sixties to go on a sprint, I can relate today's drama. It was far too hot to be walking, let alone running around the place. Unfortunately, as it turned out that's exactly what happened.

Having told Kerryn I was just popping to the beach at the end of the road for a quick dip to cool down, she warned me that we are going out to see a friend, Corrine. "Be back in ten minutes," came the firm instruction.

We are three doors down from the beach and good friends of mine, Dave and Brenda, live at the end. We developed an instant friendship worshipping at the church of Leeds United. As I walk past their garden, I see the gate is open and through the gap I spot two old dogs laid on a sun lounger. Both dogs are old and frail and both are owned by their daughter who had dropped them off for their parents to dog sit for a couple of days. I think nothing of it and pop for a quick swim. Returning up the street I find one of the dogs, Monty, has ventured off the sun lounger and is stood outside the gate surveying the world beyond Dave and Brenda's front garden. He looked suspiciously like a dog planning an escape.

Human and dog eyes lock. Monty, in his canine imagination, senses danger and decides to make a break for it, sprinting past me in a bid for freedom. There is a moment of indecision as I am caught between two options. Alert Dave and Brenda or give chase. With classic human indecision I end up doing a bit of both. First, I rush to their front door banging desperately to raise the alarm but no response from the dog sitters within. Retrospectively this was clearly a tactical error as I had given Monty a head start. I grabbed a lead hanging on the wall and sprinted down the road, slamming the gate shut behind me to avoid a second escapee who remained asleep on the sun lounger.

What follows is a desperate twenty-minute pursuit up West Coast Highway in the punishing heat. Cars halted in both directions, Monty, with a strange loping gait, moving along at speed weaving between the vehicles. He was followed, not closely enough, by a retiree running in a world of pain sandwiched between impending heat stroke and a heart attack. You can imagine that the vision of an old bloke in his boardies was not a pretty sight for the poor sods who were just out for a scenic drive on a hot Sunday afternoon. I called desperately to Monty, who did not break stride but looked over his shoulder, gave me a glance which said, "fuck that" and carried on. I waved apologetically to motorists who had stopped. Some smiled, some sounded their horns, others threw expletives through open windows. Various comments coloured the air as I passed the parade of stationary cars. "Silly old c@@t," "farking idiot," "poor man," "poor dog," "maybe he's got dementia" and "what a shame."

Eventually, Monty, seeing his evil pursuer is still vaguely in the chase, nips into a side street. I doggedly (no pun intended) followed him, but he was still twenty metres ahead.

Reminiscent of a scene from Starsky and Hutch, a car screeches beside me and the driver, a swarthy man of middle eastern descent (not sure where exactly but thank God Alfie wasn't with me) shouts for me to jump in. Close to passing out, I complied tamely, and he drove the car at speed past Monty and performed a handbrake turn five metres in front of the startled and now exhausted geriatric dog. Monty's escape route had been blocked.

I get out (I was going to use a verb such as sprung or leapt but that would have defied credibility) and in a desperate bid for freedom Monty back tracked past me. I may be slow, but I'm way too clever for him and expertly lasso him around the neck with the dog lead. He jerks back half choked. I grab him and in a final act of defiance he bites me on the nose. The trip back to the house in the car is fraught with tension as I maintain my grasp on Monty in the front seat of the middle eastern bloke's car, wearing no seatbelt. Above the sound of the 'no seatbelt' warning alarm, the driver (not the dog) barks orders to make sure I keep the rabid animal away from him. It seems he doesn't really like dogs and seeing the blood trickle from my nose there was nothing in this experience that would make him change his mind.

I won't dwell on the relief on the faces of Dave and Brenda and their gratitude when we returned the errant Monty. Their daughter would have disowned them had Monty come to harm. However, Dave felt moved to comment that Monty was half blind, had no teeth and was lame in one of his rear legs. I felt this slightly took the shine off my heroic actions.

But c'est la vie. I returned home an hour later. Kerryn not best pleased but once I had gathered my breath to explain, she was suitably sympathetic. Did I sense the slightest hint of pride in her expression or did she just have wind. She is, after all, a vegetarian.

DAY SIXTEEN

Dave popped round with a cheap bottle of wine to thank me, once again, for my heroics the previous day. I don't drink wine but probably could find a use for it when cooking. Apparently, Monty slept for twelve hours after the incident but was in good health. Well as good as an old, blind, lame dog with no teeth and incontinence can be.

Dave had a secondary motive for his visit. Having taken up golf when he retired, he asked me if I would care to join him and his pals. No pressure, low key, just a bit of fun so to speak. Initially I kept my thoughts to myself, but I got the firm impression that, as he was a beginner of only eighteen months standing, Dave was looking to recruit a member of the group who was a rank beginner. In other words, someone he could beat, like me.

I politely explained my reticence which by the end was more of a rant. I had said all my life that there was no way on God's earth that I would ever play the game. It's not a proper sport, it's played by reactionary old farts wearing ridiculous clothes and to play it is an admission that you are two steps away from your grave. (Playing lawn bowls is one step). Someone described golf as a pastime that spoils a good walk. I would not be caught dead with a bag of golf clubs and mixing with self-satisfied, elitist tossers (half of whom, smugly, conduct their 'businesses' on the course). The whole thing filled me with dread. No way would I play golf.

Dave looked at me blankly, not expecting that outburst, so I finished off by saying "of course I'll give it a go."

Kerryn's dad had given me his clubs. He has no legs ('lost' in Vietnam courtesy of a land-mine) and his shoulders were buggered. I assumed the length of the clubs were not adjusted for the fact he was a wheelchair user, but who knows if it would make any difference for an absolute beginner. It'll be a handy excuse when they see how crap I am and gives me a bit of a 'get out' with Dave who is a quietly competitive when playing sports.

When I opened our front door to see Dave out, the chorus of 'Simply the best' floated across the air. Erin, next door, was practising for her final retirement gig and giving old Tina Turner a run for her money. She'd had three previous 'final' retirement gigs. You can't keep a good woman down.

DAY TWENTY-ONE

Okay. Let's agree that this is not going to be a daily diary. Checked the mail. Another TAP leaflet. Well, it was the same one as previously posted so they must have had a quiet couple of weeks and are living off the reflected glory of past sales. For no explicable reason I decide that after two years of leaflets it's time to take decisive action. I suppose before I joined the invisible ranks of the retirees, I just mindlessly took the TAP leaflets out of my letter box and transferred them straight to the bin (recycled waste fyi, for the 'green' nazis amongst you).

As it happens, their office is about a hundred metres away in a small local shopping centre so, with nothing urgent to attend to that morning, I took myself off there.

I asked the bright and breezy teenage receptionist if I could see Mister Timewaster (remember I have adopted Timewaster, Annoying and Pointless as a pseudonym for legal reasons so, to be clear, that wasn't his real name.) Apparently, Mister Timewaster was at a Home Open but Mister Pointless was available. Miss Annoying was present in the premises but in a meeting.

Having politely enquired as to the reason for my visit, the receptionist produced her best attempt at a smile. It looked very forced as smiles go, perhaps she is also a vegetarian. I replied that it was a private matter but my teenage adversary behind the desk was no pushover. I also responded in the negative to her supplementary enquiry when she probed further by asking if I was a prospective buyer. And, as she persisted, I gave the same response when asked if I was looking to sell my property. "Oh! are you an estate agent then?" she asked with tenaciousness I secretly began to admire. The Germans wouldn't have got past her if she was in the trenches during World War One.

I told her I was retired. Her face dropped.

I was getting nowhere fast until Lady Luck graced me with her presence along with Mister Pointless who came out of his office and, seeing me engaged in a verbal battle with the teenager, asked if he could be of any help. I handed him a piece of paper which he took from me and read. Given my poor handwriting, I'd typed out my list and printed it. The only problem being that the only working cartridge in our home printer was a sort of pink colour. So, the list was not easy to read and Mister Pointless squinted but, to his credit, he battled on. On reflection I am not sure if the squint was precipitated by the colour of the ink or the contents of the list. For the record, my list was as follows.

1. Took Alfie for a walk.
2. Alfie had a shit, so picked it up.
3. Went home, I also had a shit.
4. Collected the post.
5. Played golf.
6. Cleaned the car.
7. Cooked dinner (Fish Curry)
8. Washed the dishes.

Paul Coates (8 Beachton Street)

Scratching his brow then running his hand through heavily gelled hair, Mister Pointless announced that he did not understand what was going on. I explained that I had listed my achievements for the day so I could, in some small way, reciprocate his kind efforts over the last two years. Still perplexed, Mister Pointless shrugged. Further elucidation was required so I told him that I was referring to his leaflets which kindly informed me of the houses he had sold. Politely, I admitted that I did not give a shit how many houses he had sold and therefore did not require regular updates. I added that I would appreciate it if he stopped filling my post box with his unsolicited leaflets. To fill the awkward stunned silence, I informed him that I already assumed that being an estate agent he would be selling houses, so therefore the leaflets were, at best, redundant tree killers.

Now Mister Pointless was no pushover and was not going to be bested by some senile pensioner without a fight. He explained that the purpose of the leaflet was to let me know that, should I wish to sell my house, TAP could be of assistance. My rejoinder to his offer was along the lines that if I wanted to sell my house I would ask and, for the record, he would be the last estate agent I would approach.

His gander was up and he inhaled noisily whilst scanning my list. 'Well Mister Coates,' he countered, 'it's hardly an amazing achievement to, as you so nicely put it, take a shit. Now, is it?" Triumphantly, he glanced over to the receptionist and gave her a smug wink to indicate that he had dealt with the issue and put the silly old sod in his place. Expressionless, she stared at him whilst chewing gum in a bovine manner.

I also was expressionless when I answered him. This bloke was a rank amateur at banter. He had his hands on his hips indicating that he claimed victory in our verbal exchange and the matter was now closed. I begged to differ and responded.

"You say that Mister Pointless, but at my age constipation is the ever-present enemy so I must disagree. I must counter your premise and state for the record that having a shit is no mean feat when well into your sixties and probably far more difficult than selling a house in this suburb. We are all aware it is very much a sellers' market."

The receptionist failed to suppress a giggle which annoyed Mister Pointless enough to manhandle me out of the office with a promise that no further leaflets would be delivered to number 8 Beachton Street.

DAY TWENTY-EIGHT

If you have been paying attention you will have noticed item five on my list of achievements presented to Mister Pointless.

No?

Clearly you weren't playing attention, but I'll remind you. It's playing golf. I'd played my debut game a few days ago with Dave, Nick, and Les. The first thing I learnt is that golf in Australia has a different vibe to England. Befitting a country with no frills that doesn't stand on ceremony, golf here is a different ball game. It's a game of the people. Despite the tired, dated, club bar (19th hole in golf parlance) having the grandiose name of the Gleneagles suite, the public course was picturesque but not as well kept as the posher private members Karrinyup Country Club up the road. During the week, our humble little course would be populated by an eclectic mix of retirees, schoolboys bunking off from a nearby private school and tradies who dominated the fairways on Friday afternoons. The standard was low, so it was perfect for the likes of Dave and me.

They broke me in gently with a nine-hole game. Or so I thought until I learnt that all their games were nine holes. It was not intimidating at all. On occasion our round would be temporarily halted by another golfer wandering onto our fairway to hack his ball towards us in a vain attempt to get back onto the parallel fairway he was supposed to be on. Two female octogenarians followed us behind and politely waited when we held them up. Unlike us, they hit the ball straight whilst we (particularly Dave and I) would spend a fair bit of time in the woods. Nick and Les had a lot more years under their belt and had played golf for half of their lives, so were noticeably more capable.

Not that it's important, but my debut score was sixty-six which is amazingly good for a full round, the problem being it was only for half a round. Dave's score was sixty-three, bemoaning that he had not improved one iota in his eighteen months of playing the game. But I could see he was clearly glad to finally have someone in the group he could beat. Nick, who recorded all our scores announced that he had scored fifty-two and Les apparently won with a fifty-one.

I did reflect, when alone with Dave, that Les's final score was surprisingly low particularly in reference to my personal experience at the fourth hole. It was a par four where he announced a score of six for Nick to record once he had putted out.

It didn't add up. I had found myself in the woods after teeing off with Les alongside me in a slightly worse position. It took me two shots to get back onto the fairway whilst Les hit a tree with his second attempt and found himself on the adjoining fairway at one point. Five minutes and an undisclosed number of strokes later he joined me on the edge of the green. It seemed to me that Les delivered a minor miracle with his alleged six when it eventually took me eight shots taking a far more direct route to the hole. Dave explained that Les's scoring was as optimistic as his mathematics was lacking. Which was surprising really as he is a retired accountant.

DAY TWENTY-NINE

Apparently TAP have sold a house in my street. I assume the leaflet was delivered before Mister Pointless's instruction not to deliver leaflets to my house had filtered down to the lower echelons of this corporate monster. For this reason, I did not immediately get wound up. How's the serenity? It's good, assisted by the dulcet tones of Erin next door channelling her best Gloria Gaynor and beating out 'I will survive.' More serenity watching the rolling waves of the Indian ocean. Sipping my tea, I watched four surfers bob on the waves. No attempt was made to catch one.

Next to me Alfie was patiently sunbathing in his favourite spot on the balcony awaiting an opportunity to bark at his next victim who had the impertinence to traverse his part of the street. It didn't take long and nearly gave an old bloke a heart attack who couldn't immediately ascertain the location of the threat as Alfie was three metres above him.

Not a lot else worthy of note happened which is why my diary is not a daily activity. Oh! I should mention that I wrote on TAP's latest leaflet which announced their successful sale. My note read, 'In your face, you useless set of c@@ts' and I posted it into the letterbox of Smug and

Worthless (SAW). You've guessed it, it's another pseudonym for the direct competitors of TAP. SAW also have a small office in our local shopping centre two doors down from TAP.

I forgot (accidentally on purpose) to sign my name underneath the comment I had scribbled on the leaflet. I do hope that the people at SAW won't jump to any conclusions regarding the author. It would be truly unfortunate if they were to wrongly assume it came from their neighbouring estate agents, just because it happened to be written on a TAP leaflet.

'Ahem.'

'That would be awful' whispered Mister Schadenfreude in my ear.

DAY THIRTY-THREE

On occasion I go for a walk with Dave and Brenda which is an exercise opportunity and a way to discuss the big issues of the day. In this case the latest news on Leeds United in the transfer market.

Very little progress regarding the Leeds United situation and it was not the most successful of our walks mainly because we did a workable impression of the three wise monkeys. You know. See no evil, hear no evil, and speak no evil.

Unfortunately, Brenda was fresh from the doctors where she had had a biopsy taken from a small lump on her throat and could not talk for three days. Dave on the other hand was two days off an appointment to have his infected blocked ears cleared and had a kilo of cotton wool stuffed into each ear. He could not hear a word. Alfie, who always followed us closely behind, had a minor eye infection. All in all, the whole walk resulted in what I can only describe as unsatisfactory.

We walked; I would ask a question or make a comment. Dave would say "Eh!" whilst Brenda would attempt some half-arsed version of an imaginary sign language that she had devised.

She clearly thought that the signs she was giving, whilst silently narrating what she was saying in her brain to accompany them, were comprehensible. She did not seem to appreciate that we did not have access to the thought narration in her mind therefore interpretation was far more challenging than she imagined. I would just nod to her to indicate that I understood and shout at the top of my voice to Dave which drew strange looks from other walkers who clearly assumed I was engaged in some form of elder abuse. The only silver lining was that Alfie, with his eye infection, could not see very well and one of the regular walkers, a black labrador, escaped Alfie's racist wrath as he trundled past us.

Probably the only highlight of the walk was when Brenda suddenly broke out into what can only be described as a workable impression off Muhammed Ali's shadow boxing. Dave shouted, 'What on earth are you doing Brenda?' and I confess to initially being totally dumbfounded. It took five minutes but, as it turns out, it was worth persevering because, unlike the walk, this result was highly edifying.

What my mute friend was telling me was that she had been over to the shops to get some Brussel sprouts and a packet of laxatives (yes, I know it's unnecessary detail but that's what happens in conversations with other retirees) and witnessed a heated argument in the offices of TAP. Every unit is sectioned off with glass, so the place resembles a collection of fish bowls. Apparently, Mister Worthless, was gesticulating wildly and vigorously waving a leaflet in the face of Mister Timewaster. In response, Mister Timewaster was using the 'F' word encouraging his competitor to vacate his premises with all due haste.

Something, Brenda waved and shrugged in her incomprehensible sign language, had clearly annoyed them. It might have been the leaflet, she surmised. I thought she had probably hit the nail on the head. Brenda thought the whole scene was highly unprofessional. I agreed with her vehemently, whilst holding my own counsel regarding what may have precipitated this conflict.

It was my turn to hear, see and speak no evil.

DAY THIRTY-FIVE

There has been a major coup in the golfing group. Nick, who steadfastly refused to attend any public course other than our usual one, had been persuaded to, for one game only, shift the competition to an alternative venue. Marangaroo golf course is a little better maintained, a little further to drive to and, frankly, a welcome change. I particularly liked it because the kangaroos hang out there and it is all quite enchanting. I never thought I would ever write the words 'quite enchanting' as they belong in a Famous Five book or a Disney film rather than the rantings of an old bloke. But there you are, I squeezed it in, so respect to me. Eat your heart out Enid and Walt.

Sorry I digressed there.

Unfortunately, the kangaroos were less enchanted when Nick tee'd off. He gave an almighty swing, and the ball hurtled at speed but faded alarmingly right towards the trees hitting a kangaroo on the head. The poor beast fell over but eventually hopped up (no pun intended) seemingly without any long-lasting damage. I bring up this event, not to upset the wildlife enthusiasts amongst you, but to discuss God.

With Dave, Les, and myself on the atheist side of the fence, Nick is a catholic or at least claims to be. He says he is a practising catholic, so I assume he is not particularly good at it and there is room for improvement. I began to wonder whether his belief system was giving him a competitive advantage. Whenever Dave, Les or I drive off badly (a frequent occurrence) the trajectory of the ball veers towards the sylvian elements of the course (i.e. the trees) as does Nick's. However, the said ball, if owned by Dave, Les, or me, studiously avoids any trees on the boundary of the fairway and lands deep into the woodland. Often, our balls are nestled at the bottom of a tree trunk, or worse, a Balga Grass Plant (more commonly known, by those who are politically incorrect, as a 'black boy'). Not so with Nick. Nineteen times out of twenty, it will hit an object on the boundary, usually a tree not wildlife, and bounce benignly onto the centre of the fairway. We have termed this as 'a Frazelle.' Which you may have guessed is Nick's surname.

This inevitably brings up the query as to whether Nick has been to church that morning as it happens far too often to dismiss divine intervention as a cause. This time the kangaroo's head is the agency that diverts Nick's ball from a certain quadruple bogey to a potential par as it comes to a halt nicely sat up on the edge of the fairway. Not only that, but it is also on the right-hand side, lined up perfectly for negotiating the dogleg to the left.

Now I have had much intellectual discourse over the years with friends who believe in God. I often say at the end of our debate that we are not that far apart in our belief systems. In this instance I, as an atheist, am surprisingly close to my friends who are catholic. How so you may ask? Well, comes my rejoinder, on planet earth humanity is diverse and believes in thousands of Gods. As a catholic you have dismissed all these thousands of Gods as false and determined that they do not exist, as have I.

Where this leaves us is that I may disbelieve in say 4,957 Gods and you, as a Catholic disbelieve in 4,956 having decided that the Catholic God does exist. The difference is marginal, one in almost five thousand. The only difference being that I do not believe in one more God than the Catholics. So, I conclude, we are actually remarkably close on an intellectual level. All that said, as I play golf and the 'Frazelles" mount up game by game, I silently reconsider whether I am on the wrong side of the 'does God exist?' fence.

DAY THIRTY-FOUR

It's a Sunday afternoon and I walk back into the house to be greeted with the same enquiry that Kerryn makes every Sunday. "Are you injured again?" To which I proffer the same response as I limp towards her. "Yes I am."

A friend contacted me some weeks earlier to enquire as to whether I would be willing to re-invigorate my football career and play for the Subiaco Shakers over 55's team. After much thought and soul searching, I agreed. My friend was in dire straits as this was the club's inaugural team for that age group and they were struggling to find enough ambulant people of that vintage, who were willing and able to participate. I guess my first problem was that the league allowed for teams to have four players between the age of fifty and fifty-five which meant that for the most part I was attempting to keep up with men who are up to sixteen years younger. I can tell you that it's a lot to give away when you have passed the mid-sixties age point.

The next question in Kerryn's now predictable line of interrogation is, "Did your team win?" At least on this query I could respond positively and informed her that we beat Wanneroo City two nil.

Question three always references back to question one, lest I think I have escaped scrutiny. “So how did you get injured?”

I respond. “Kicked by a snowman.”

Now unlike you, Kerryn knows what I am talking about. Early in the season, I labelled a certain type of player as a snowman. Picture a quite large snowball placed on a much larger one - which is your basic structure of a snowman. Keep this visual in mind. Well in this league there is a type of player whose complexion is very pale, whose head is very bald and whose torso is very rotund. Most hail from north of the border (if you live in England) in a wasteland named Scotland. For some yet undiscovered reason, Scotsmen over here of a certain age who choose to play football are aggressive and incredibly angry. Perhaps if I was unfortunate enough to be born in Scotland I would be as well.

Wanneroo City had two, Scotsmen that is. One in attack and one in defence. Both shouted, screamed, complained, whinged and berated the poor referee into submission whilst all the while kicking lumps out of our legs and elbowing my teammates in the face. They don’t seem to have grasped that it is a Sunday league of old blokes kicking a ball around in the deep shadow of their glory days. Nor do they grasp that they should just simply be grateful that they have sufficient degree of movement to participate in a game. It is not the

Premier League nor the World Cup. If it was the latter, no Scots would be participating anyway.

This behaviour persisted for the first twenty-five minutes until eventually we scored. What typically happens, as it did in this case, is that they turn their anger towards each other and spend the remainder of the game fighting amongst themselves. However, this happy event did not happen until I already had a growing bruise on my thigh and pulled a calf muscle attempting to avoid a second kicking. Like an old dog about to be put down, I shuffled towards the sanctuary of the touchline and ended my involvement in the game after twenty-four minutes.

Twenty-four hours later I would be at home feeling as though I had been hit by a truck and unable to dress myself without even the capacity to slip on my, tent like, underwear from a standing position. I laid on the bed and did a sort of shuffle to get the jocks in place. Socks are always the biggest challenge, and I had to sit on the edge of the bed and bend awkwardly to hook them onto my foot. The underwear and sock process ends in a flop backwards to catch my breath followed by a comforting rest laid on top of the duvet with Alfie next to me engaging in a sympathetic nap. Oh! the trials and tribulations of an elite sportsman.

DAY THIRTY-NINE

I am on the local sports ground and It's a Friday afternoon having been asked to help with the local under-tens footy team. That is Australian rules football, not proper football.

For the uninitiated, Aussie rules, or footy as it is known in Antipodean circles, is a unique sport played in only one country in the world. Its rules defy logic when compared to other ball-based team games of a similar ilk. I can only describe it as cross-country assault (the pitch, sorry oval, is expansive) with the incidental involvement of a slightly undersized rugby ball.

The rules, where they can be explained, add to the uniqueness of this game. For example, you get a point for missing the goal providing you only just missed it. If you kick or punch the ball out of play it doesn't go to the opposition (as in soccer, rugby, hockey etc.) but it is thrown back in play by an umpire. Unless, and here is the catch, the umpire thinks you did it on purpose. So, a degree of mind reading is required. If the umpire has read your mind and determines that you kicked/punched/headed it out on purpose, then the opposition is allowed to kick, not throw, the ball back in. Heading the ball is allowed but everyone will take the piss. You can use your hands and feet to progress the ball and even carry it for a few metres (but not too far in the umpire's opinion or it's a penalty). The opposition can leap on top of you and wrestle you to the ground.

"Why cross-country assault?" I hear you ask. "That last bit about wrestling to the ground sounds no different to rugby."

Well, here is the thing. If you take a long run up and leap on top of an opponent's back, shoulders or head whilst trying to catch the ball, it is deemed to be acceptable no matter how badly you injure the other player. Consequently, half the players on the pitch (sorry oval) end up receiving a flying knee, Bruce Lee style, to the back (or back of the head in some cases) which frankly would be deemed illegal in an UFC bout, let alone a ball game. However, as with all rules in this game there is a "but." It's a different matter if you fail to grasp and control the ball in the air, in which case the opponent gets to take a free kick providing his back is not broken and he is not concussed. If you are awarded a free kick following this assault, a teammate will take the kick for you whilst you are being stretchered off and rushed to the nearest hospital.

I won't go on with a list of other examples because I could write a book on it but let me make one final comment. If a player is disaffected or so annoyed with an opponent that he swings a haymaker rendering that player unconscious with a broken jaw, the team that gets penalised is the one which has the player with the broken jaw. That player gets taken (stretchered) off and his team find themselves a man (or woman let's not be sexist) down. The budding Mike Tyson is allowed to stay on the field for the remainder of the game and may or may not get punished retrospectively the following week, depending on how good his (or her) lawyer is. There is no guarantee that he will get off the pitch (sorry oval) alive of course if the other team seek retribution when play recommences. Local hospital accident and emergency departments tend to be quite busy during the footy season.

DAY FORTY (WRITING ABOUT DAY THIRTY-NINE)

I got so wrapped up explaining the intricacies of footy (Australian Rules Football) that I forgot to record what happened yesterday when helping with the under tens training session. Before I recount the events, I should explain that the North Beach reserve is home to many sports including footy in the winter and athletics in the summer.

My friend and the coach, who was an ex-professional footy player, was late, so I took the little tickers onto the pitch (sorry oval) for a warmup. I told them to jog round the edge of the oval to get the muscles working and watched their progress until my eye was caught by a large muscular gentleman (or brick shithouse) stood in the concrete circle on the edge of the oval. It was, for clarity, a discus throwing circle from where they project a deadly two-kilogram metal disc during the athletics season. For further clarity, it was not the athletics season. For yet further clarity the nets of the circle, used to prevent lethal projectile flying sideways into the heads of unsuspecting passers-by, were not yet up. Athletics season was not officially due to start for six weeks. I walked over to Mister Brick Shithouse until I was about ten metres in front of him. He picked up a discus to prepare to throw and then noticed me standing in the planned flight path of his weapon.

I politely requested that he desist from his activity lest he decapitate one of the tickers. I pointed to the group circling the oval who were now running back towards Mister Shithouse. Seeing that I was conversing with the behemoth, the group stopped running and formed a sort of protective huddle.

"You need to move out of my fucking way mate," said Mister Shithouse in a very menacing tone.

I explained that I would not be moving. I further explained that he needed to depart as it was not athletics season. It was footy season, and the kids had the right to be using the oval. He adopted the 'I was here first' argument and made it crystal clear that if I did not move, he would come over and re-arrange my features. Three of the tickers burst into tears and, given I have had a good life which was far nearer the end than the beginning, I felt both sympathy for the children and a degree of serenity at my fate. So, inexplicably, I stood my ground. With Churchillian rcsolve I told him I would not be moving.

He then adopted a more righteous approach. "Look you old c*@t, I am doing this for the likes of you. I devote hours of my time to do this, to bring the likes of you old bastards some reflected glory."

Against the background of renewed crying from the tickers, I politely explained that what he was doing was dangerous, out of season and he needed to leave. I refrained from using expletives due to the proximity of the tickers.

He took a step forward, neck veins bulging and shouted, "I'm a bloody professional athlete mate. If I qualify this month, I'm gonna be representing your country you ungrateful dickhead. I need to fucking practice so move, or I'll take your head off."

I explained that, unless he was English, he wouldn't be representing my country so I did not give a toss and, pointing to the discus, added, nor should he.

Having resigned myself to a hospital visit, I instructed the kids to do another circuit. They did not need to see the horrors of my bloodied and beaten body and I could see my friend in the distance making his way towards the oval. The cavalry was coming but probably too late. When I turned to face the discus gorilla, I was taken aback at the sight of him packing up his weapons. He then marched off in the opposite direction, giving me the finger over his shoulder.

"Everything okay?" enquired my friend. "The kids look as though they've been crying. Have you pushed them too hard?"

"No. All good." I replied, "but I'm feeling a bit unwell so perhaps you can excuse me."

"No worries, mate, I'll take over from here," said my friend. He was slightly concerned at my possible ill health but quickly became preoccupied with the tickers.

I went home for a Grandad nap. It had been a challenging day, and it was only two thirty in the afternoon.

DAY FORTY-FOUR

Loud and persistent banging at the rear of the house. I peer out of our scullery window which overlooks mad Stan's yard which is to the rear of Erin and Bernie's house. Mad Stan occupies a house which looks onto West Coast drive. It is prime land worth millions with extensive ocean views but the house (I use the term loosely) sitting on it is borderline derelict. His garage, which adjoins the rear of our property only has half a roof which, to be fair, is more than the room attached to it has. I have no idea what the original function of the roofless room was, but it is now jam packed with rubbish and assorted detritus. Contents range from damaged bicycles, rusted gym weights, a car engine, and a pile of wooden tennis racquets to what looks like a functioning sound system from the 1970's. Tables and chairs are piled high and the whole space is full to brimming.

Occasionally Stan will remove the padlock on the door to squeeze more newly acquired items into the space. Given the lack of roof and windows, one could be tempted to question the efficacy of padlocking the door at all. Especially as it is practically hanging off its hinges anyway.

Mad Stan suffers from Plyushkin's disease. I looked it up and it is defined as a mental disorder characterised by persistent difficulty in parting with possessions and engaging in the excessive acquisition of items that are not needed or for which no space is available. There you go, you've learnt something new. Unless of course you are a psychologist.

Dave told me the other day that he (Stan not Dave) had walked up to a nearby suburb, Carine, to collect and carry (the four-kilometre distance back to his home), a broken sun umbrella and stand. It was advertised as free in the Quokka which is a local rag surviving amongst the last vestiges of printed media.

Mad Stan has been described in many ways. A selection is listed below:

1. A few sticks short of a bundle
2. A few cards short of a deck
3. An elevator that doesn't reach the top floor.
4. Only one oar in the water
5. One prawn short of a cocktail
6. A sandwich short of a picnic

I think you've got the picture. And don't ask me what he was banging and why. He had a hammer in his hand and seemed to be knocking seven bells out of a large metal drum of indeterminate purpose.

DAY FORTY-FIVE

Today was a day to reflect on whether I co-habit with a bunch of racists.

I took Alfie to the park for his walk and doing a circuit of the main oval passed a fenced off area which is designated for dogs. Many dog owners use the area as a sort of social hub for dogs and, to be honest, themselves. Alfie and I are firmly of the view that at least fifty percent of the dogs and their owners are mad. All that barking, snapping, and fighting. And the dogs aren't much better.

Alfie, being of the view that he is human, turns his nose up at the very thought of entering the area. Believe me, I have offered him the opportunity several times by holding the gate ajar for him to join his canine cohort. But he seems hell bent on avoiding entry at all costs and just looks at me like I am an idiot and walks on. On occasion, some of the lower orders (other dogs) rush up to the fence to say hello to him as he passes. Occasionally he will deign to stop and give a doggy hello through the wire. Today two perfectly friendly dogs, a labrador and a poodle, both trot up happily to say hello but he dispatched them with a threatening snarl. You've guessed it, they were both black.

When I got home, I was going to recount the story to Kerryn, but she was in conversation with Jake (my manchild giant of a son) and his mate Josh and Josh's mother who had just dropped him off. Now Jake (my fourth child, aged eighteen, so still at home) is six foot four and loves basketball as does Josh. Josh is a mere six foot eleven and has been recruited by an American college to play in their team. The reason I did not recount my park story is that Josh and his mother are Nigerian. I think you get the picture now.

Anyway, Kerryn spent the whole conversation calling Josh's mother Justice. To be fair having myself lived for a few years in Africa I know that this type of name is not uncommon. What may be a noun to us, is a pronoun to others. When she left, Jake asked his mother why she was calling Josh's mum 'Justice,' when her actual name was 'Success.' Kerryn, to be fair, was mortified. I guess, to give her the benefit of the doubt, at least she opted for another noun (as opposed to a proper noun) to demonstrate her cultural awareness and that she was on the right track.

DAY FORTY-NINE

Living his best life on the balcony, Alfie was lying still, eyes half closed. It's a tactic he uses to lure passers-by into a false sense of security. Like a tightly coiled spring being released, he leapt into the air and started barking furiously. I had only been on the phone for thirty-three minutes but was hopeful that, having gone through twenty sub menus, a human would eventually appear on the line. I was attempting to find out why my water bills had trebled from the previous period by speaking to a human directly, where emails had failed.

I am not a total luddite and tried to use the robot on the website called an Auto Assistant. It was, as it turns out, just designed to give you hope and tease you without providing anything like a useful answer to my question (s). I had typed in several responses to Auto Assistant's questions, as it tried, unsuccessfully, to understand the nature of my enquiry. However, Auto Assistant clearly couldn't assist, and I found myself going in circles. Ironically, I was answering far more of the bloody robot's questions, than it answered for me. I was beginning to wonder who was assisting who. Eventually it gave up and told me to call an 1800 number. Hence here I was over half an hour older listening to banal lift music whilst being told, periodically by a speaking robot, that my call was very important to them.

As it turned out, Alfie's latest barking attack was not racially motivated but may have given me insight into a possible cause of my latest water-based dilemma.

Leaving my mobile phone on the kitchen bench playing 'It's Raining Men,' (music to keep punters like me amused whilst they waited for hours), I rushed to the balcony to see the source of Alfie's angst. I was just in time to see the car drive off, having mounted our front verge and destroyed our sprinklers. We were now the proud owners of a mini fountain which was flooding our native plants which were designed to survive the intense heat and live on minimal water. I rushed downstairs and outside to switch off the reticulation before Noah came along with his bloody Ark and snatched up Alfie to join his female counterpart.

Once I had returned upstairs (our living is upstairs as I have mentioned) I grabbed my phone. Clearly it had been answered and, not getting a response at my end of the line, the customer service person had ended the call.

Never mind, I now had bigger fish to fry.

I searched for 'Deluded Cow' in my list of contacts, pressed the call button and instantly a female voice answered with a curt "Yes."

"Hello, Jade, this is Paul,"

"Yes, I know. Your name came up on the screen. What is it?" came the frosty reply.

"It's about Imogen, she has just driven over my sprinklers for the twentieth time."

By way of very brief background, Imogen is the same age as Jake, they were in the same class at primary school and Kerryn became friends with Jade, Imogen's mother, until they grew apart. Personally, never was a big fan of mother or daughter. Helicopter mother and entitled daughter who went through a series of friends all of whom were dumped. On every occasion poor Imogen was being bullied. It was of course nothing to do with Imogen being a 'you know what.' Unfortunately, they live in a nearby street and occasional interactions are inevitable.

In a voice that would have grated Parmesan cheese, Jade snapped back in defiance. "Well, I doubt it was my Imogen. How do you know it was her? She gets blamed for everything."

"I think the main clue, Jade, was that the car drove off our verge at speed, barely under control and unless you know anyone else who has a pink Suzuki Swift with the registration 'Princess1', I think I am relatively solid ground in accusing her."

"Were there any other witnesses?"

"Yes, Alfie can testify."

"Very amusing, I'm sure. What do you want me to do about it?"

"Well Jade, you should give your daughter more driving lessons. God knows who you bribed at the test centre. And, also, perhaps you could arrange and pay for the replacement of my sprinklers."

The phone went dead, so I assume that was a 'no.'

DAY FIFTY

I may have mentioned that I am a lifelong supporter of Leeds United. Last Christmas Kerryn bought me a couple of comedy garden gnomes dressed in Leeds colours (all white) holding up Leeds United signs. I put them on the front verge. They are quite small and tasteful – as much as gnomes dressed up in football kit can be. Well, they are quite small at least.

It's a sad day as I leave the house with Alfie for his morning constitutional and discover one of the gnomes has been crushed into a pile of powder. Imogen is the prime suspect, but I have no proof.

I need to consider whether this is an act of war.

On my way to the park, I pass Jade's house and see the pink Suzuki Swift parked outside. Is it my imagination or is there a smudge of white powder on the front wheel arch on the driver's side.

DAY FIFTY-FIVE

I hobble up the stairs to our living area and am greeted by Kerryn's usual three questions to which I have responded, 'Yes I am injured,' 'No we lost seven-two' and 'My bad knee gave up on me.'

As for the seven two loss I think the team we played looked like they had an average age of just over forty or they had all lived very wholesome lives. So, they either cheated or have found the fountain of youth in their suburb, Joondalup. A suburb known for being mainly inhabited by POMs (people born in the UK). Frankly, I was grateful to be injured and left the field after thirteen minutes. I am too old to be playing against people younger than my oldest child.

I mentioned my bad knee, and old age has provided a never-ending litany of physical issues. As a younger person who would visit a GP once every five years on average unless I was taking one of the kids, I used to be very intolerant of the older generation who I thought were hypochondriac timewasters. Nowadays, I am beginning to creep into the group I once despised. The GP junkie. The person, usually of my vintage who visits the GP every week with one complaint or another. I now find I wake up each morning with something new. Frankly if I attended to every issue, I would have to rent a room in the GP surgery.

However, in the case of my left knee I felt this issue merited a visit. Not to the GP but to the Physiotherapist. Our leader and captain Gary asked if I was okay as I left the pitch, but I could not really hear him because each step I took was accompanied by an audible click of my knee joint.

DAY FIFTY-SIX

Went to the Physiotherapist following the recommendation of a friend whose son played sport at a high(ish) level. So off I went to Hosty. Surname Host but in basic Australian colloquial parlance one added the 'y.' It's usually either a 'y,' an 'o' or an 'ah' that is added when assigning nicknames in Australia.

Apparently, Hosty was a very good physio, but I found it hard to judge. What my mate did not tell me was that Hosty didn't stop talking. He was clearly very knowledgeable but would reference, nonstop for the half hour I had paid for, past and current client's injuries. Sixteen minutes into the session and we had not addressed my issue at all, but I felt I had a good grasp of the diagnosis and prognosis of selected clients even if their injury bore no relation to mine.

The common Hosty denominator was that no matter what the issue, surgery should be avoided, and rehabilitation was the only way forward to strengthen the muscles around the injured area. Every second sentence would reference his thirty-six years' experience. He was also very insistent that a scan would be expensive and not tell him anything that he didn't already know from his, you've guessed it, thirty-six years' experience. But apparently if I wanted to waste money getting a scan, then that was up to me. With casual self-confidence he would throw in the comment "it'll only confirm what I already know but it's your call." It felt like being at a poker table, I had a good set of cards, but did I want to call Hosty's bluff and risk losing (wasting) hundreds of dollars on an unnecessary scan.

Having learnt the prognosis for half the suburb who use Hosty, I ventured to move the conversation to my own immediate needs by asking what his conclusion was regarding my own clicking knee. "Well, let's put it this way," he said with a smile, "I wouldn't swap my knee for yours. Yep, I wouldn't want your knee."

So, I went away without getting a scan but with a program of his exercises and none the wiser as to the nature of the problem. Though I did gain, as I have said, an intimate knowledge of everyone else's problem who had visited him.

DAY FIFTY-EIGHT

Two days of Hosty's exercises and the clicking has disappeared. Hosty is a bloody genius.

DAY SIXTY-ONE

Woke up this morning to find a sign on our front lawn. It was a sign stolen from a house sale in the neighbouring street. Most of the original words had been crudely painted over with white paint to provide a suitable background for the message that the culprits wanted to convey. In black letters they had painted the names of the teams which participated in the recent AFL Grand Final with the score. Kerryn's team had lost, and this was some attempt at amusing banter.

The identity of the culprits was no mystery. They were friends, one of whom followed the victorious team. Over the last two years there had been a low level, but persistently ongoing, prank war. For the sake of privacy let me refer to them as Dumb and Dumber. Recently I had given Dumber a birthday card with a lottery ticket inside. He scratched the ticket, and it told him he had won $5,000. He was jumping for joy around his living room whilst explaining to me what he planned to do with the winnings (a trip to Sydney). Eyes watering with tears of joy, he thanked and hugged me.

I felt shit.

To be honest I have never felt so bad about a prank (and I have done a lot throughout my life) as in that moment. His expression of dismay, when he read the ticket closely, will be forever etched in my mind. I am never, ever, buying a packet of prank lottery tickets again. I threw the rest out.

Nevertheless, like the Mafia, there is a code to be followed even in dealing with your enemies. And, like the Mafia, it was a "no-no" to involve family in business. They had crossed the line and attacked Kerryn, mocking her team's loss. Retribution was not an option; it was a necessity.

DAY SIXTY-TWO

Dumb and Dumber came round to gloat at their latest escapade. Kerryn, who is a far better person than me, laughed good naturedly as they acted like a couple of pork chops shouting on our front lawn and pointing at the sign. We decided to leave it up for a couple of days before dismantling it. They had obviously gone to some effort, including breaking the law, so it only seemed respectful to give their efforts a degree of longevity.

I pointed out that this clear act of aggression would obviously precipitate an appropriate response. They did say that there had been a degree of karma already. In the act of stealing the estate agent's sign from a client's lawn, the very same estate agent was driving past. For the record it was Mister Timewaster. At the sound of screeching Audi brakes, Dumb and Dumber had to escape through a nearby reserve called Star Swamp.

Kerryn and I laughed at their story, but I assured them that, regarding the matter in hand, a proportionate response would be forthcoming. Off they trotted, lambs to the slaughter. I turned to walk back inside and Kerryn asked where I was going.

"To make a sign of my own," I replied.

DAY SIXTY-THREE

Checked the post today and there was a leaflet from TAP, but this was not a glossy one. It was more a strip of paper with a few words typed on it. It was basically a whinging letter referencing the (previously mentioned in the Dumb and Dumber episode) theft/vandalism of one of their signs which not only resulted in a financial loss to TAP but was upsetting to the client involved. It offered a small reward for information which led to the identification of the perpetrators of this heinous crime. 'Heinous' is my (sarcastic) word, not those written on the leaflet. On this issue I sided with Dumb and Dumber rather than TAP.

There was also a parcel delivery, some other mysterious item ordered by Kerryn. I'd given up asking what the parcels contained years ago. Alfie's barking on the balcony was particularly intense so I assumed it was being delivered by Mister Mutunga. Ushering Alfie back from the balcony edge with my right foot, I gave an apologetic and hopefully friendly wave to continue my campaign to build bridges. Mister Mutunga gave a tentative half-hearted wave back from inside the sanctuary of his lorry cab. Alfie is not easily deterred and squeezed through my legs to get to the balcony barrier to resume his barking at poor Mister Mutunga. Shaking his head, Mister Mutunga drove off.

I had given some thought to Alfie's racism. I mean, it's practically impossible to train or convert a human racist, so what's my chances with a dog. Out walking today, I got talking to another dog walker who owned a poodle. Apparently, her dog is racist as well. Maybe racism is a race thing if you know what I mean. Alfie is part poodle part cavalier so maybe, just maybe, all poodles are racist just like Germans and South Africans.

And yes, incidentally, I recognise that the irony of calling a whole race racist, is that this is racist. So, who am I to talk.

DAY SIXTY-FIVE

Have just watched a documentary on body language. Very interesting but not entirely convinced as to the veracity of what appear to be some very subjective assumptions on the meaning of twitches, ticks, hair strokes, and eye movements. I thought half of what they said was a load of bollocks but decided to put what I had learnt into practice. I felt that having watched the full hour of the documentary I was now something of an expert.

Went over at the shops to get some provisions and put my newfound skills into practice. I didn't intend to pop into TAP but passing their offices on the way to the supermarket, the temptation was too strong. As soon as I walked through the door, the face of the teenage receptionist dropped (do overt negative facial expressions count as body language?). I, on the other hand, sported a cheery smile. Although it was clear from her expression that she didn't want to, she asked if there was anything she could do to help. I replied that my query was in relation to a recent leaflet I had received which had piqued my interest. She folded her arms, which I know in terms of body language is not particularly a positive sign.

Guardedly, she replied that they had ceased, at my request, delivering leaflets to my home. I confirmed this was the case but assured her that I was referring to the one which referenced the theft of one of their signs. She got defensive saying that this doesn't count. It was not a leaflet but more a slip of paper prepared for the interest and benefit of the local community. To both reassure and placate her, I nodded in agreement with arms out and palms pointed skywards.

My open body language worked, and she unfolded her arms and enquired as to the nature of my query regarding the leaflet (sorry slip of paper). When I said I was intrigued to know what they had in mind in terms of a reward, she re-folded her arms with a suspicious squint (not sure if a squint counts as body language). Leaning back in her chair she asked, warily, why I wanted to know. Did I have some information? Palms out, facing the receptionist this time, I re-assured her that I didn't have any information yet (I hope touching my eyebrow didn't give my dishonesty away) but that I have a fair bit of time on my hands, being retired and all. I explained that if the reward was financially worthwhile, I would be happy to devote some of that time to investigating the crime. Strictly on a 'no win no fee' basis, I re-assured her with more open palm gestures.

She explained that the reward was a voucher that entitled the recipient to ten free take-away coffees from the café next door. For your information, the cafe is called Ninety-Six which is the number of the address. Clearly the owner had little imagination from the marketing perspective. I thanked her but explained that I don't drink coffee because ordering it is far too complicated with the small, long, skinny, almond milk, two shot, latte bollocks. Let's be honest, it's another fucking language. Pardon my French. Why do we say pardon my French? Surely, it's racist to assume all the French language constitutes swearing.

When I got home, I realised that the reason for going out in the first place was to get provisions. I totally forgot this and trundled back to the shopping centre. This time I passed the TAP offices without entering.

DAY SIXTY-SEVEN

I've had Dumb, from the Dumb and Dumber pairing, pay me a visit. The main item for discussion was the sign he found on the rear window of the cab of his Ute. Prepared by my own fair hands, the sign was placed there so that it could easily be seen from the street to attract the attention of passers-by. Jake had followed my instructions to the letter and taped the sign there a few days ago because we knew Dumb was away in Sydney at the time. It read:

For sale. Cash only $4,500 ono. Contact number 0405 746643

The mobile number above is not Dumb's actual number obviously, I changed it here for legal reasons. Therefore, I advise that you don't try to ring it.

Apparently, Dumb had received several calls whilst in Sydney from a pushy South African who was very keen to make the purchase and offered the full asking price. This did not surprise me as, in the current market, it was worth four times that amount. The South African was not going quietly, even when he was told by Dumb that the vehicle wasn't for sale. With increased irritation and angst caused by an overly persistent potential buyer, Dumb expressed in strong terms that he had no idea what the South African was talking about but if he did not stop ringing, he (the South African) would be relieved of several teeth when he (Dumb) returned home. In response, the South African expressed his view that if some stupid c**t insisted on putting a ‘for sale’ sign on his vehicle what did the stupid c**t expect. Dumb countered with the fact that he had not put the sign up, but it was the pommy c**t who lived on the street. At this point in the conversation, South African seemingly ended the call.

All in all, it was a win for the good guys. You will have noticed that this particular mission was focussed on Dumb, rather than Dumber. You see, I still felt guilty about the lottery ticket prank so spared Dumber retribution on this occasion. I’m just an old softy at heart.

DAY SIXTY-EIGHT

Today I acquired a new hobby via the interweb, social tedious or whatever you call it. Sorry it's called 'WhatsApp.' Which I presume is a very clever play on the phrase 'what's up' as it is all about interacting with each other. Apologies again, it's not 'Whatsapp,' it's 'Messages.' It's not like the old letterbox system, is it? In the old days you just get messages in one place. In the modern world you must continually monitor Whatsapp, Messages, Messenger, Linked In, your email blah blah blah.

Anyway, I'm rambling.

I got the following message out of the blue. I repeat it below word for word but don't worry about the privacy issue. I'm sure the sender won't complain.

Sender: Hey dad just so you know I'm using this number temporarily as my phone has broken. Text me on this if you need me thanks.

Now I have come to accept that nowadays written (sorry typed) interactions are usually light on grammar, so I did my best to ignore this, but I must admit that it does slightly irk me. There was a love heart put at the end of the message which was very touching. At my age you take any affection offered on the rare times you get it. So, I responded.

Me: Is that you Simon?

Slight delay …

Sender: Yeah it is.

Imagine my excitement at discovering I had a son that I was not aware of. For clarity, I have three sons, Tom, Jake, and Bill, not to mention a daughter, Lucy. Perhaps, as is the current trend, Lucy had transitioned into a Simon. Would that make her a L, G, B, T, I or Q or a plus? Either way, I thought I'd better check in.

Me: Let me know if there is a problem.

Sender: I just left the phone repair shop they told me I have a service issue it's a fault in the device.

I'm sorry but hasn't Simon ever heard of the concept of 'commas.' He is no child of mine. I gave him a curt 'OK.'

Me: OK.

Sender: Im just going to buy a new one online a new one online.

For God's sake whatever happened to the good old contraction apostrophe and please check what you type, you've (note the contraction apostrophe I just used) repeated yourself Simon. So, I gave him another curt 'OK.'

Me: OK.

Sender: I'm looking at phones online but I can't decide whether to get the standard iPhone 15 or the plus with the bigger screen what do you think?

Like I would have a fucking clue but at least he has re-discovered the existence of the contraction apostrophe. Setting grammatical issues aside, my philosophy is you only live once (refer earlier diary entries about the existence of God). I encouraged Simon to live life to the full.

Me: Go for the bigger screen if you've got the money

Sender: Yeah your right I'm going to do that.

Two things about this bit, ignoring the comma issue. One, no child of mine has ever used the phrase 'your right' (correct spelling would of course be 'you're right') when addressing me. Two, what the hell happened to the full stop. I'm getting as bad as Simon.

I let things hang for a bit and awaited further developments. They came about an hour later. A clear mistype indicated a degree of agitation and excitement.

Sender: AaI'm trying to order my phone with my card but it keeps sending a code to my old number. If it's okay can I use your card and as soon as I get my old number back and my

new phone set up I will get the money straight back to you.

Golly, Simon's has had a run of bad luck, poor thing. Broken phone and a service issue at the same time. Now his two-factor authentication process is buggered. Should have selected the questions method. He must know his mother's maiden name, surely. So, I replied with a 'no problem' and did not respond further for ten hours as it was my bedtime. When I woke up, I sent the following message.

Me: Did you get the message from Simone. What are you twins like? You're as bad as each other. Would lose your heads if they weren't screwed on. Ha, Ha. Thought it would be safer to send my bank details to her as your phone is temporary. She will order your new phone for you. I didn't want to send bank details to a temporary phone. There are a lot of worthless pieces of shit out there trying to scam people instead of earning an honest living.

Me: PS. Simone is fictional like Simon.

DAY SEVENTY-EIGHT

Today I almost had breakfast with the love of my life at a local café called 'Little Bay.' In fact, the morning had gotten away from us, so it was more brunch than breakfast. Kerryn always goes on about the poor service culture in this part of the planet, so you never know what you are going to get in local eateries. I have to say that although Paris could give Perth a good run for its money, she has a point. 'Little Bay' did not disappoint, I can tell you.

In fact, I will tell you.

The café rests on West Coast highway giving expansive views of the Indian Ocean which on this day offered up smooth rolling waves, perfect for surfing. Away from the reef, the smooth aquamarine ocean glistened in the bright sunlight. (Got all poetic there, didn't I?)

We took a seat under a sun umbrella in the open area at the front of the café and scanned the breakfast menu. On offer was the usual fare, eggs, bacon, toast, muesli, tomatoes, mushrooms, blah blah blah as well as some speciality creations.

I looked up from the menu to see the welcoming face (irony alert) of a teenage server whose facial expression reminded me of the rear end of a pig. With supreme effort she managed to spit out a disinterested enquiry as to what we would like to eat. Kerryn ordered the Avo Smash (that's avocado on toast for the uninitiated). From the server's attitude I already had a waning appetite so requested a toasted bacon sandwich which elicited a disapproving wrinkled nose from the server. Before I could ask if there was a problem, she shot off back inside muttering that she would consult the Chef.

Kerryn gave me her look. It didn't bode well for the server.

Two minutes later the server returned and announced that they could not take our order because the breakfast session ended at 11.15am. She added as a sort of 'fait accompli' that they were now moving on to the lunch menu which would begin at midday. Seeking further clarification, I asked if that meant we had to order from the lunch menu. She replied in the positive and said she could take our order once the lunchtime session started. I asked her if she thought it was reasonable for us to sit here for forty plus minutes before ordering. I also was moved to enquire as to what happens between 11.15 and midday, to which the server replied that it gave time for Chef to organise the changeover.

During this interchange Kerryn had checked her mobile phone and chose her moment to strike. Maintaining steely eye contact with the server, who recoiled slightly (most people do under her stare), Kerryn said, "It's still only 11.10am now, so when we ordered it must only have been 11.05am. So can you ask the Chef to reconsider please." It was like the best courtroom drama where the defence presents a telling piece of evidence at the death, just when the innocent accused on trial looks like he's going to be toasted (continuing the breakfast theme) in the electric chair.

Barely acknowledging Kerryn's request, the server turned and walked back to the kitchen. She returned a minute later and announced that the Chef had generously agreed to prepare the Avo Smash but not the toasted bacon sandwich as it was not an item listed on the menu. She was oblivious to my argument that the menu had a list of side orders which included toast and bacon. Perhaps, I suggested, mimicking Kerryn's courtroom demeanour, I could order a side of toast and a side of bacon. Then, having got fully into the role of the defence Barrister, I dealt the killer blow. Perhaps the Chef could also muster his Michelin Starred skills to place the bacon side order between the toast side order and bring me a fucking toasted bacon sandwich.

Of course, as soon as I resorted to swearing I had lost the initiative and moral high ground so Kerryn intervened and said that perhaps we can order two Avo Smashes. Sour faced, the server gave me a 'and fuck you' expression, agreed to Kerryn's request and left to deliver the order to the Chef. My additional request for a side order of bacon, which I shouted as she departed, trailed behind her only to be lost in the ether.

As soon as the devil server was out of sight, Kerryn tapped me on the shoulder and stood up. We left, never to darken the doors of the Little Bay ever again. Presumably, the Chef and the server ate the two Avo smashes.

DAY EIGHTY

Had a bit of a philosophical moment Sunday evening whilst shooting the breeze with Dave outside my front door. For no obvious reason, the subject matter of our conversation and the problem we were workshopping took me back to my university days. Transported back to the late seventies I was cosseted in a small book infested room with three other students and a bald, pompous philosophy tutor. I looked forward to these tutorials even though I hated the tutor, because this small group included the source of my unrequited love. (I won't name her for legal reasons).

In that dusty room in Keele Hall (I was at Keele University), which was a sort of monument to Victorian architecture, we would discuss all sorts of nonsense that Philosophers prattle on about and normal people don't. On this occasion it was the ship of Theseus. Won't bore you with all the details but the basic premise is that a bloke in ancient Greece had a boat which he sailed to Crete and docked it there. Gradually over time planks decayed and were replaced until there reached a point where every plank on the original ship had been replaced. Plutarch (Greek philosopher bloke who clearly had too much time on his hands) questions whether it is still the same ship. Was it still Theseus' ship if none of the original ship remained?

Trust an English philosopher to put a spanner in the works. Hobbes, a dour smart-arse, said, well never mind that, think on this my old Greek fellow. If all the old planks were gathered up and a ship was constructed from them, is that not Theseus' ship? Nah nah, nah, nah, naaah.

Baldy tutor looked at me for my view on Hobbes point. However, I had been distracted by unrequited love who had just crossed her legs in boredom, although to me it was one of the most erotic actions I had witnessed up to that point in my life. All I could come up with, having not done the reading in preparation for the tutorial, was a health and safety issue tinged with a slightly valid perspective. I responded with the view that if a vessel was made from the decayed planks of the original ship, then it would immediately sink and not function as a ship. Therefore, it could not be described as a ship, let alone Theseus' ship. Baldy muttered something about my response being inventive but totally missing the point.

Anyway, I digressed, and you must be wondering what this had to do with my conversation outside the house on a slightly blustery Sunday evening. Let me enlighten you. It was the sad realisation that in my youth I would, when not in the bar, occasionally be engaged in intellectual high-minded discourse whereby I would grapple with the great conundrums of the world. I don't do this anymore which seems a waste of my age and acquired wisdom. One would think that nowadays I would be nearer to the answers to these great questions and less distracted by the beauty of youth in the form of 'unrequited' love.

So here is the thing that connects the intervening fifty years between university and the present. My high blown tutorials would last forty minutes which was the exact length of time that Dave and I had been discussing which bins we should leave out for this week's refuse collection. We had red, green, and yellow bins. Red was a given as it was for general rubbish and had to be put out every week. That's fine but which bin should accompany the red. Was this week a yellow bin collection (re-cyclable stuff) or a green bin collection (organic decomposable matter). Is this what my life as a retiree had come to? An endless circular discussion on which bin we put out. I had a solution, reminiscent of my response to the Hobbes query whereby I pulled an intellectual rabbit out of the hat. Sadly, it didn't, like my Hobbes response, quite cut the mustard.

What was my solution? It was simple but genius and Dave looked at me in admiration. Look down the street and see what others had done.

Now mad Stan had put the green bin out, but mad Stan was, well, mad. Would you place your life in the hands of mad Stan? Not me for one replied Dave. Erin and Bernie were of even less use. They had more money than the central reserve bank and were currently on a European cruise and had not put their bins out for three weeks. Looking further up the street there was a mixture of yellows and greens with one or two indecisive residents putting both out.

In the end we opted for yellow.

DAY EIGHTY-ONE

The bin men came and collected the green bins.

Bastards.

DAY EIGHTY-FIVE

Alfie's on the balcony, head slightly twisted and ears pricked listening to Erin's singing. She has been melodiously bashing out a medley of songs about cities in Europe. We've had 'Tulips in Amsterdam,' 'Vienna' (not Billy Joel but Ultravox) and 'Barcelona' by good old Freddie Mercury. Luckily, she didn't attempt 'Niggas in Paris' by Jay Z and Kanye West or that would have set Alfie off. Clearly, they had enjoyed their European cruise. Bernie has settled himself in his favourite chair on the front patio chatting to all and sundry who passed by. He looked up and gave Alfie a wave, who responded with a friendly bark whilst wagging his tail.

On our other side of our house, Erin and Bernie's grandchildren were laughing and playing in the small pool that Micheal, Bernie, and Erin's son, had installed during their house build. It was all quite idyllic in the street. That is until Imogen came racing down in her pink killer car, music blasting, oblivious of anything else on the road. This time she narrowly missed my Leeds United verge gnome, which was the replacement for the last one she destroyed. Was it worth another phone call to her mother Jade. No, I decided, it would be a futile exercise and why spoil the peace.

DAY EIGHTY-SIX

I may have already mentioned Kerryn's hatred of summer in Western Australia. Along with her main nemesis, the heat, there also comes another lower grade irritation. Little Athletics.

Now I can sense you are wondering how on earth a bunch of little tickers running around the grass can cause a grown woman, who incidentally is also a parent, any level of angst. Truth is, it's nothing to do with the little tickers gambolling in the summer heat. As far as Kerryn is concerned they can gambol with abandon whilst their moronic parents watch them getting exposed to the damaging sun for hours on end. Let them all soak up the ultraviolet radiation to their hearts content. It is not the kids; the main problem is adults who lack self-awareness.

In this case the main guilty party is the announcer whose incessant narrative through a high-powered sound system floats across the field, down our street and into the bedroom every Saturday morning. Unfortunately, Kerryn's combination of noise sensitivity and a strong yearning for a sleep- in after a hard week at work finds this activity highly stressful.

We are now into the third week and requests to the council to instruct the Little Athletics cult to turn the sound system down to a level below that which AC/DC require for their average concert, have fallen, ironically, on deaf ears.

Time for direct intervention.

I find myself amid gambolling tickers and associated parents staring across the desk at the announcer. I am trying to conduct a reasoned conversation in between her announcements. No mean feat. You have probably guessed, but it didn't go well. My initial enquiry as why there had to be so many, in fact constant, announcements was met with derision. I pointed to a copy of the program of events on her desk and argued that every parent has this program so why do they need countless announcements. 'So what?' came back the reply.

My gander was up, and I responded in kind. 'So little Oliver, and little Oliver's parents, must know exactly where he should be, and at what time, when the three-legged sprint, egg and bloody spoon and sack race was being run."

Missus Announcer responded curtly that they only had proper bona-fide athletic events, not egg and spoon races, and these meetings were serious occasions. I responded that may be the case but does everybody involved possess a lower-than-average intelligence. Or illiterate, I added, tapping the program.

Missus Announcer repudiated my assertion that she loved the sound of her own voice and that her constant flow of instructions was unnecessary and over the top. Then she made an announcement which boomed through the speakers informing the under nines that they had to gather at the western end of the field to throw the discus. This momentarily threw me as my PTSD kicked in triggering the memory of Mister Brick Shithouse. But I recovered quickly and went back on the attack.

I resumed with a reasoned alternative. How about turning the volume down, came my suggestion. There was no way she was going to dampen the sound of her own voice, and this was dismissed as untenable because the little tickers (my words not hers) would not hear. I then asked if these meetings were being held for the partially deaf because from the comfort of my bed half a kilometre away, I could hear every word with absolute clarity. She countered by blaming the weather. The wind apparently must be carrying the sound. If that's the case I rebutted, then the wind is also carrying it past the miniature athletes and therefore the sound volume can be turned down. Her frown indicated an internal struggle to grasp a further counterpunch, but none were coming.

She told me she had a lot of announcements to make and could I please bugger off.

Reading the writing on the wall, I did.

DAY EIGHTY-NINE

Kerryn made the mistake of venting her frustration at the Little Athletics noise pollution to two of her friends who happen to have the misfortune to be married to Dumb and Dumber. This morning outside our front verge was, another, sign they had stolen. It was in the shape of an arrow with the words 'Registrations for Little Athletics Here.' It presumably was placed outside the administration office at the oval some weeks ago. Had they placed it in front of our house some weeks ago it might have been funnier and more effective. At this point in time, the season is well underway, and registrations are closed. It was, therefore, a bit redundant. That did not mean, of course, that this latest act of aggression could go unpunished. Oh no, no, no, my friends.

I saw Dumber in the street, and he was very pleased with himself. I pointed out that their repeated use of signs as a weapon smelt of being a one trick pony. He smiled and his inner joy could not be quelled. I would bide my time, wreak vengeance, and dampen that joy.

DAY NINETY

I cannot believe I have got to day ninety and not mentioned that Kerryn's parents live in the same street. So, I had better give them a bit of airtime to cover myself in the unlikely event that either of them reads this.

Understanding how Kerryn's mind works has been a journey but the key to understanding a person can often be found in the observation of that person's parents. With Kerryn as my partner I am blessed in many ways. For example, I do not ever need to worry about having arguments about who is right and who is wrong - because Kerryn is always right. This marvellous trait can be seen within her parents, particularly her mother Noelene who will never hesitate to judge and inform you of where you are going wrong. This wisdom can be imparted on any subject or topic ranging from how to boil an egg to the correct way to bring up your children. For the record, an egg takes three minutes and forty seconds and raising a child a little longer.

Now her father, Graham, is a wheelchair user who lost his legs in the Vietnam war. I do love this euphemism that people use. He, of course, did not lose his legs whereby he could later recover them from where they had been misplaced. They were blown off him courtesy of a landmine. As a couple they have faced and overcome horrendous challenges in life because of what happened to them in their twenties. In my book, Graham and Noelene must be admired for that. So, who cares about the small stuff.

I wrote this little pearl of wisdom above as Noelene sits on the couch telling Kerryn the necessity for our son Jake to study for his exams. Clearly the implication of lax parenting is being aired. Noelene, of course, has no idea of the extent and effort that Jake has been putting in because she does not live here, so I calmly keep my distance. For the record Jake has been surprisingly diligent, far more so than myself at his age and I must admire his efforts. Kerryn who is always right on all things except those where her mother is righter (not sure that's a word), sits next to Noelene turning an unhealthy shade of red and looks ready to blow a gasket.

When her mother leaves Kerryn treats me to forty minutes of exasperation and mis-placed blame. Mother and daughter don't speak for a few days.

Alfie twists his head and pricks up his ears trying to ascertain the source of his mother's anger. He hopes it is not connected to the fact that he chewed one of her new shoes because he was bored and we dared to leave him alone, unentertained, for two hours this morning. I know this because I went into our walk-in wardrobe to put on some shorts and saw the chewed remains of the left shoe hidden in the corner. We boys need to stick together and there is no way I was going to 'dob' him in.

DAY NINETY-TWO

Was invited by Graham to a fund-raising quiz night which was being run by a charity called 'Wheelchairs for Kids.' It is a charity that relies on an army of volunteers, average age seventy-eight, which focusses on the construction of wheelchairs from spare parts which then are transported to third world countries. I won't insult your intelligence explaining why this resonated with Graham. As an ex-politician and Minister in a Labour Government, Graham has the profile and lived experience to be the ideal Patron.

I was sitting at the table with Kerryn and her friends from her university days who come together for these type of events. There is a slight generational difference as I am eleven years older than Kerryn and her friends. I mention this because a brief exchange made me think about humour and political correctness through the ages.

All tables were instructed by the compere to write the name of their teams on the answer sheets which led to a fevered discussion amongst our team. We were on table eleven and one bright spark suggested we call ourselves 'Legs Eleven' aka the bingo call. I reflexively, because you will have guessed by now, I am a smartarse, suggested a better name, given the event we were at, might be 'No Legs Eleven.' Now this group managed to laugh, gasp, and look horrified all at the same time. Had they been a lot younger I think I would have been kicked off the team and in modern parlance, 'Cancelled.'

Now here is the thing. Every succeeding generation has its rules and for the most part I personally believe that, overall, we are slowly progressing. There is much greater inclusivity for the diverse population we are and how we define ourselves. However, as with all generations, there is the Nazi element that, contrary to their stated desire to be accepting of all, are not. The current trend is to 'Cancel' those that don't follow the new set of rules creating an environment of fear and censorship not unlike the authoritarian societies they supposedly despise. Those in the public eye, politicians, entertainers, comedians etc. live in fear and many clever, talented people become gagged, which diminishes their talent and what they bring to the world.

Of course, humour can be challenging and, of course, the racist, sexist discriminative jokes are shocking and appalling. But the real issue is what the intent was. Does the person saying it, really mean and believe it. Is that what they really think? Did I really think it is funny that children are being killed and maimed by landmines? Of course not.

Graham has achieved amazing things and has the respect of his peers. Some of those peers, especially the ex-military ones who shared the horrors of war with him, gave him a nickname. What was his post landmine nickname? Well, it was 'Stumpy.' Now it is easy to castigate his peers and 'Cancel' them, but to do so is an act of pure ignorance if you have not considered a whole range of circumstances. Not least the period and environment they were born into, their life experience and their true nature. These men risked their lives for their friends and in Graham's case saved his life and dragged him to a helicopter and to safety. Humour can be dark and often the darkest can be the funniest but ultimately it is just words. It's not a landmine. If you found yourself in Graham's situation bleeding to death in a foreign land, who would you want by your side? The men who gave him the nickname 'Stumpy' or the modern keyboard warriors.

DAY NINETY-FOUR

A successful response to the recent unprovoked attack from Dumber (junior member of the Dumb and Dumber partnership) was delivered today. Dumber drives a cement truck and digging through a plastic box full of paraphernalia I found a packet of joke parking tickets. There were three, each consisting of an outer plastic wallet (very like the real thing I have to say) and a ticket which is placed inside the weather protective wallet. The ticket has a space to fill in where you could write your own reason for the traffic violation. Admittedly it was a very low-level response, but I still have vestiges of guilt from the prank Lottery ticket affair.

After scribbling my 'reason' for the offence on the ticket, I slipped it into the wallet and walked up the street to place it under the windscreen wipers of his truck. By way of relevant background one or two neighbours had complained in the past about where it was parked (i.e. on the street rather than the driveway).

I was enjoying a morning cup of tea on my balcony whilst Alfie barked at a pensioner dressed all in black, when Dumber roared past in his truck. To my surprise I could see that the ticket was still in place, lodged under his wipers. He clearly had not seen it. Later in the day there was a knock at my door which I opened to find the clueless features of Dumber staring at me.

He recounted the events of the day where he had unloaded cement at the site of a new build house in a suburb called Carine. After unloading the cement, he left the truck on the street whilst he walked over to a nearby Deli to get a pie for lunch. The builders on site promised to keep a look out for traffic wardens who were active in the area. On his return he saw the parking ticket and lost his temper. After swearing at the house builders who denied seeing any traffic warden, he marched over to the truck and snatched the ticket from under the wipers. He waved it at them shouting 'well what the fuck do you call this you bunch of idiots?'

Apparently once he read the ticket inside, he had two pies to eat. One was Steak and Mushroom the other was Humble.

For the record, the message I wrote under the heading of reason for the parking fine printed on the docket was simply, 'Being a dickhead.'

Advantage moi. Dumber to serve.

DAY NINETY-FIVE

I was sitting on the balcony watching the surfers who were not surfing. Waves were obviously not worthy of the effort. Seamlessly transferring from a canine doze to a rabid alert attack dog, Alfie leapt off the sofa and skidded to the glass barrier as a delivery van pulled into the driveway. From my position I could not see the lorry once it is parked but I hear the cab door open followed by the swish of sliding doors. I waited for Alfie to explode but his response was far more muted than usual. It was more of a warning bark than the usual vitriolic effort.

Hope springs eternal. I think to myself that maybe, just maybe, Alfie has turned the racism corner. This was definitely an improvement and a major step forward. I got off my chair to peer over the edge to acknowledge Mister Mutunga particularly as my efforts over the last few weeks had thawed what was previously a cold war.

Looking down I could only see the top of the delivery driver's head as he carried the parcel to my front door but judging by the skin tone of his bare forearms, he was distinctly Caucasian. I shouted 'hello' and the driver looked up and smiled. I thanked him and enquired after Mister

Mutunga. Apparently, he was on leave visiting relatives in Kenya.

I started to tell Alfie that he was a good boy for not barking too much. It's all about positive re-enforcement. (I know that because I'd just seen three minutes of a program on TV about dogs who behave badly.) He twisted his head in that way he does but was distracted before I could finish the sentence and ran rabidly to the barrier. He barked with such vehemence that the physical effort caused him to break wind. A pensioner dressed in black walked by with her black Dachshund. Much more work to be done on the dog cultural training front.

DAY ONE HUNDRED

There is an annual event at the bottom of our street which brings hundreds of people to the small beaches in our area. Parking becomes a free for all and the local council have employees marshalling and controlling proceedings. This event took place today.

To many, the flesh from the Abalone mollusc is a delicacy. Personally, although I love seafood, I can take them or leave them. I am certainly not going to get up early and scrabble around fighting the hordes to get the allowed quota of what amounts to a handful. The scramble and free for all can, and has, resulted in deaths. The Asian community in particular go mad for these things and despite the best efforts of the local authority marshals, the carefully drafted rules of engagement are studiously ignored. As are the published warnings about being ocean safe.

It seems to me that the resources that go into policing the process and the costs of damaged verges where cars are carelessly parked do not justify the end result of a few free shellfish for each person. If you add to this the increased danger to road safety from illegally parked cars and the potential loss of life, you've got to wonder why it is allowed to go on. A significant proportion of 'fishers' are, as I said, Asian.

Judging by the injuries and life-threatening incidents over the years, this community in particular needs protection. Thank God for our Surf Life Saving community.

Watching the parade of bedraggled Vietnamese, Koreans and Chinese locals walking up the street with full bags, which look suspiciously like they have exceeded the council's quota, Alfie remains silent but interested. Looks like he is a fan, and his racism doesn't extend to Asian ethnicity. Perhaps he wouldn't be so understanding if he knew what appears on the menu in their homeland.

Having said that, the Swiss are partial to a bit of Fido as well, but the Swiss are few and far between in Perth. Not that I'm judging. Just trying to be sensitive to Alfie's feelings. One man's pet is another man's main course. Or in the case of the Hindu's and the English, one man's sacred symbol is another man's national dish.

DAY ONE HUNDRED AND FIVE

Woke up with every bone and muscle in my body aching. A friend who lives up the Street, Natalee, formed a team of beach volleyball players. A local league was set up and games played on sand courts created just beyond the greens at the North Beach Bowling Club. Probably should have joined the bowling club because the activity and people are, in my case (and Brenda and Dave's) more age appropriate.

The inaugural evening did not go too badly with our team of five comprising Natalie, one of her male friends, Dave, Brenda, and myself. We ended with a win and two losses and my quite effective technique of heading the ball, channelling my football skills, caused some amusement. Our choice of name did cause some consternation with the organisers because it is too long to fit into the tournament's computer application. In the end the Beachton Street Budgie Smugglers had to be shortened to Smugglers, which lost the humorous element as well as making us sound like we were wannabe pirates. Most of the other teams are considerably younger with a fair bit more energy, but as a team we gave a good account of ourselves.

DAY ONE HUNDRED AND SIXTEEN

Dave delivered some sad news today. He told me one of his daughter's dogs died. Given the way he belittled my dog saving heroics by describing Monty as toothless, old, blind, and partially lame, I assumed the worst. It was however Hank, the other dog, who was also old and, unlike Monty, had the good grace to stay put whilst his compadre made his bid for freedom that fateful day.

Monty's apparent indestructibility brought an old TV show to mind, which I watched when I was a kid. Captain Scarlet. He was a bloke who fought the evil Martians and acquired their ability to retro-metabolise (which is presumably not a genuine biological process) to justify the fact that, like Monty, he was indestructible. I am surprised it was not banned. It was quite violent for little tickers like me and became progressively worse as the writers of the show would find increasingly innovative and bloodthirsty ways for the Martians to destroy Captain Scarlet. Every week he would get shot, blown up, eaten by a shark, or crushed by a large vehicle or landslide. Without fail, he would pop out the other end, unharmed. By a twist of fate all Captain Scarlet's associates had a colour codename. Had Alfie been around at that time I can picture him rushing to the screen every time Captain Black appeared.

On the topic of heroics, the reason I have not written an entry for several days is because Kerryn, the boys and I went on a five-day break to Singapore. One day whilst availing ourselves of the treats in the clubroom of the hotel, I heard a groan. There was a private area, sectioned off with a glass partition and through the window I saw an older woman, in her eighties laid face down with three hotel staff rushing around her in a state of panic. I told Jake and his mate to follow me and went to assist. Having calmed the woman and assessed if she had broken anything – she hadn't – I then brought in the two strapping six foot five manchildren to help get her to her feet and rest her in a chair. Meanwhile, a hotel staff member came rushing in with a first aid kit.

It is at this point in the proceedings that the generational and cultural differences became most apparent. Like a true Gen Z, Jake grabs the first aid kit from the Singaporean staff member (who culturally defers to him out of politeness), rifles around in the contents and pulls out an item. With the utmost certainty, Jake tells me that this is what I need. I can only admire the confidence of this generation and their ability to speak with knowledge and absolute authority even when they are totally wrong. I tell him that what he has in his hand is an elasticated gauze leg bandage which will not be required for the lady's bleeding nose.

Having ensured everything is hunky dory, including the now bloodless nose, I ushered the boys out so we could leave the lady and the hotel staff in private and thought nothing else of the matter. On our next visit to the club room, we were greeted with a deputation to honour our presence which I can tell you did little to arrest the self-confidence of Jake and his mate. For the remainder of the trip we were greeted with the prefix, 'Most valued guests.'

And the lady? What I did not mention is that as I attended to her, she exclaimed 'scheize' as she laid bleeding face down. Now, if I had realised, she was German, then …

DAY ONE HUNDRED AND SEVENTEEN

"Isn't it your court date tomorrow?" was Kerryn's opening comment for the day as I prised open my tired old eyes. I reached over to the bedside table and switched on my mobile to check the date. It's harder to keep track of dates when you're retired.

After squinting for a few seconds, I replied in the positive. (My reading glasses were characteristically in a place where I least needed them i.e. not in the same room as me – I am sure there is a mischievous spectacle goblin in the house).

The incidence that precipitated my appearance in front of the local judiciary occurred prior to the commencement of my diary writing, but what can I say, the wheels of justice run slowly. So, as I will be making an entry tomorrow to report the outcome of my trial, I had better get you up to speed.

About six months ago I was driving in East Perth looking very respectable in my suit. It was one of the final days of my working life. Minding the road and my own business I reached down to the console to put my wallet back into the well as it was teetering on the edge and about to fall.

Whenever items go between my seat and the central console they are lost forever. It's one of those unsolved mysteries of the universe.

My thoughts and inner peace were invaded by the jarring sound of a police siren, and I looked in my rear-view mirror to find a motorcycle cop gesturing for me to pull over. I was on a large busy road, so I drove on for fifty metres until I reached a side street which I turned into and pulled up.

I got out of the car to find an angry looking and, how can I put this politely, slightly portly cop whose mid-section was placing considerable strain on the lower buttons of his shirt. He shouted at me, admonished me for not immediately stopping and did not accept my reasoning regarding the circumstantial road safety issues. My own anger was now matching his, although I was wisely keeping it contained within. In my dotage I had matured and on occasion could keep my smart mouth in check.

He insisted I was using my mobile phone.

I insisted I wasn't.

More words were exchanged with neither party giving any quarter. His aggression led me to the presumption that he had had a bad day. One might think he had pulled over the Yorkshire Ripper as opposed to an old bloke who he was alleging committed a minor driving infringement.

He wrote out a ticket and handed it over, but the die was cast. I told him I wouldn't be accepting this, and he said derisively that he would see me in court. As he clumsily mounted his motorcycle, the swinging of his leg over the machine was slightly impeded by his gut, he barked a final order that next time I should stop immediately. Thankfully, my retort was drowned out by the guttural roar of his motorcycle as he fired up the metal beast of justice. Had he heard my response there would have no doubt have been a further charge of wilfully obstructing a police officer with offensive language.

My gander was up and when I received the notice of infringement in the post, I completed Part G of the form entitled 'Court Election.' I filled in the section confirming that I was the driver and have elected to have the matter dealt with by the court. Various paperwork followed including the summons where I indicated that I would be conducting my own defence. I have to say that these forms all carry all sorts of threats which may discourage an innocent man (or woman, let's not be sexist) from challenging the law. The paperwork, in a rather matter of fact way, informs you that false declarations could carry a five-year prison sentence. Seemed disproportionate to me, I'd have probably got less if bonked the fat copper on the head with a crowbar.

With six months to prepare, including watching as many courtroom dramas as I could, I was ready to go. I particularly liked ‘My Cousin Vinnie’ and thought I might model myself on Joe Pesci who played a newly qualified lawyer who specialised in personal injury claims. He is asked to defend his impoverished and wrongly accused cousin in a murder case, but the defendants do not realise that Pesci’s character is devoid of experience in serious criminal cases. Marisa Tomei is superb in this incidentally, and I highly recommend it.

But I digress.

Suffice to say I had studiously gathered evidence, prepared a file outlining my defence and I was ready to face judgement and take on the full force of the law.

What could possibly go wrong?

DAY ONE HUNDRED AND EIGHTEEN

My day in court had come. Suited up for the first time since I retired, with my black file in hand, I entered the hallowed corridors of the Magistrates Court of Western Australia, 510 Hay Street, Perth. When my turn came, I walked into the courtroom past a huddle of cops. I believe the proper collective noun is a 'force' of policeman but there are of course many less complimentary terms including adopting the name given to a certain group of farmyard animals. In this case, the 'force' seemed to comprise of a prosecuting sergeant, the fat motorcycle cop and a junior one who looked as though he had barely left kindergarten.

Fat cop was full of himself. I heard him joke, as I passed them, that it would be over in a couple of minutes which would be good because he fancied a coffee (and no doubt a couple of doughnuts). Kindergarten cop chuckled. Given the elapsed time and the doubtless hundreds of tickets he had subsequently issued, Fat cop did not realise that the short, big eared old bloke who had just passed them was the defendant.

Four other cases were heard before mine, but they were a quick procession of guilty pleas for minor offences. Two were for drunk and disorderly, one for minor assault and the fourth one for petty theft of a Mars Bar. With all four cases there was no hearing as such, and the magistrate passed judgement with the look of a bored teenager sitting through a double period of mathematics on a Friday afternoon. I was to be last in the queue as I was the only one who had the bare faced cheek to challenge the allegation against me and take on the might of the Western Australia legal system.

With all the preliminaries over, including confirming that I was me and I would be defending me, the magistrate invited me to say my piece. She looked about ten years younger than me and had the careworn but earnest look of somebody who has spent too much of their life dealing with dickheads and the detritus of society.

I opened my file.

My first comment was that I was innocent of the charge and that the Fat cop was mistaken. I pointed to him as I said this for dramatic effect, like in 'My Cousin Vinnie.' Obviously, I didn't call him Fat cop. I used the word' Constable.' Now the pronunciation of 'constable' with a northern English accent could sound even more pejorative than calling him Fat cop. The Northern English 'o' can sound like a 'u' – but let's not go there).

With a sigh, the magistrate asked if I had anything further to add to support my innocent plea.

I replied in the affirmative.

She sighed again.

I explained that I was driving with the windows up because it was raining and that the Constable (pointing over to him again) could not have had any clear vision through my side window which was covered with rainwater. I handed out a Bureau of Meteorology report confirming there was rainfall in East Perth at the time of the alleged defence.

The prosecuting sergeant rose, objected, and said I had not submitted this documentation prior to the hearing. The magistrate asked me if this was the case. I replied that I did not know I had to. She asked me if I received instructions and information on procedural matters from the police. I said I was given no guidance whatsoever.

She glanced over to the sergeant with what I perceived to be mild admonishment. The sergeant could neither confirm nor deny that I had been sent the appropriate paperwork required for those conducting their own defence. Nevertheless, whether admissible or not, I had already got the magistrate slightly on my side and the point about the rain, which is incidentally rarer than hen's teeth in Perth, was made.

"Is there anything else Mister Coates?" asked the magistrate assuming there wouldn't be.

There was.

She sighed again.

I reached into my file for the charge notification. I asked the Fat cop who was sitting with the sergeant, how old he thought I was. "No idea," he replied petulantly, then hazarded a guess. His guess fell short of my true aged by eleven years. I felt slightly pleased at this unintended compliment but maintained my concentration and professional demeanour.

"Is this relevant?" asked the magistrate.

I went on to explain that the charge sheet has several errors including my date of birth which placed me twenty years younger than my actual age and the address printed had the wrong house number. This, I suggested, indicated that the Constable, who I felt was agitated and aggressive at the time, was prone to error on the day and therefore was mistaken in what he saw.

The prosecuting sergeant scoffed and muttered something about a minor admin error. To regain the upper hand he asked, sarcastically, "Well what did he see in your hand if it was not a phone?"

I replied that it may have been my wallet which might, from a distance in poor visibility with rain on the car window, look like a phone.

The prosecuting sergeant scoffed again. He said most men keep their wallets in their pockets and pointed out that I was wearing a suit which surely had plenty of pockets. My story sounds unlikely; he told the magistrate.

I replied that I don't put my wallet in my suit pocket because bulky items put the trousers out of shape and that spoils the line and look of the suit. I explained that I carry my wallet and phone around and this was in the central console.

"Unlikely," repeated the sergeant.

At his point I delivered a serious blow to the prosecution. With a fortunate stroke of serendipity, I had carried both my phone and wallet to the stand and placed them on the ledge of the witness stand. I lifted my wallet and phone above my head for dramatic effect. With direct eye contact to the magistrate, I declared that it was plain to see that I had carried these items to the stand and not placed them in the pocket of my suit trousers.

I awaited a gasp from the gallery, like you get in films, but all I got was another sigh from the magistrate.

"Is that everything Mister Coates?" enquired the magistrate, hopefully.

"Only one more thing. If I may Your Honour." You can see I had done my homework on the correct parlance. Seeing her impatience, I did not want to get her offside, so I added, "It will only take a moment as I am conscious of the court's time." That was another phrase I had heard in film court dramas.

I declared that I wanted to submit records of my mobile phone which indicated that I had neither received nor made any calls at the time of the alleged offence. Nor had I sent or received any messages, therefore I had no reason to even touch my phone and, furthermore, it confirmed I had not used it. The prosecuting sergeant had seen the writing on the wall and did not even raise the complaint about failing to submit my evidence prior to the hearing. He barely looked at the copies handed to him. In fact, there was a clear two hours of no calls or messages at the time I was stopped. This was not so much a killer blow on the legal battlefield but stabbing those already dead.

"Before I make my judgement on the outcome of this case, may I ask Mister Coates what you do?"

Well, that was game set and match. Once I described my role as CEO of a Charity that supports families with chronically ill or disabled relatives, it was all over. She had heard enough.

Her judgement was case dismissed being that it amounted to my word against that of Fat cop. All the police could offer was Fat cops' word and the evidence I presented in support of my word, whilst not conclusive, placed reasonable doubt on what was alleged.

I became the only person in the State of Western Australia with a hundred percent success defence record in court.

Eat your heart out Joe Pesci, I didn't even need Marisa Tomei to bail me out.

DAY ONE HUNDRED AND NINETEEN

Basking in the sun and glory of my recent court win, I was on the balcony couch, sipping on a refreshing cup of tea with Alfie laid dozing beside me. Somehow, the laws of physics were cheated when I managed to avoid pouring the scolding drink into my lap after Alfie leapt off the couch to bark rabidly at a passing black labrador. When his nemesis had passed and he calmed down, I was surprised he did not return to the couch to resume sleeping duties. Instead, he stood and stared whilst a delivery van pulled up and he gave it a low-level guttural, almost dismissive, growl. I peered through the glass barrier of our balcony to see Mister Mutunga carrying a parcel to our front door.

Was this a development and improvement in the racist behaviour of Alfie? Uncontrolled barking and aggression turning to a mere growl. I thought not and concluded that it was more a case of familiarity breeds contempt rather than a shift in racial tolerance.

It was actually a good job he did not bark because, as Mister Mutunga pulled away, I was able to hear the faint noise of a man calling out in the distance. It took a couple of minutes to discover the source, but I realised eventually that it was coming from the ocean, and I thought I could see a head bobbing in the water. I grabbed my binoculars and focussed in on the bobbing head. It was a man who had chosen to swim in the (dangerous) area near the Tom's surfing spot. Your average Australian would know that this is not a good idea, especially with the rip tide that was visible. The swimmer looked middle eastern, and, I assume by the naivety of his chosen swim spot, he was a tourist.

Not believing my ears and eyes I called Kerryn to get her opinion. Was he in trouble or had he chosen to observe the Zuhr prayer whilst swimming. It wasn't a call infused with panic; there seemed to be an air of resigned fate and acceptance. Being middle eastern I guessed he might be Muslim. It was, after all, around noon (that's when the Zuhr prayer is delivered by the Muslim worshipper for the benefit of the non-Muslims amongst you). Apparently, I was over thinking the situation, and Kerryn immediately rang the surf life savers. Long story short, the man was pulled out of the water minutes later and taken to a waiting ambulance. Reports are that he was shaky but okay. Kerryn had done her bit to save the day.

This superhero lark is getting ridiculous. Firstly, Monty the dog, then the octogenarian German, and now I am saving people whilst sat on a couch drinking tea, admittedly with a level of superhero delegation to Kerryn in this case. Probably not so much Superman but Superannuation Man.

DAY ONE HUNDRED AND TWENTY-SIX

It's beach volleyball night again. For the last couple of weeks, we have been predictably mediocre but not entirely a push over. Dave and I are reasonable, though admittedly ageing, sportsmen and Natalee was the World Champion at Wave Skiing. Yeah, I'd never heard of it either but, having seen it on the internet, that's an impressive sporting CV. However, this week we had a secret weapon. What is more impressive than the world champion sportswoman you already have on the team, you may ask. Well in this instance, an Olympic Gold medallist at beach volleyball.

Natalee who obviously moves in the rarified atmosphere of sporting superstars has a very good friend called Kerri Pottharst, who came over from Sydney to stay with her. Google will confirm her credentials and our results that evening were much improved. Though her glory days has passed some time ago, Kerri proved too much for the opponents who, being of a much younger generation, did not recognise who the old bird, with an impressive spike, was. However, one sharp onlooker did. The following day the local rag reported the guest appearance of the former Olympic champion at the humble North Beach courts. The Beachton Street Budgie Smugglers had left their mark on the tournament. Thank you, Kerri.

DAY ONE HUNDRED AND THIRTY-ONE

Though not an original thought, it seems to me that in older age, birthdays become less meaningful. In fact, you try to ignore them. With the march of time, you become more conscious of your mortality and a birthday, with a defined number, is something that cannot be argued with. This led me to thinking at what point in older age is it significant enough to merit an excuse for an almighty piss up.

Sixty-six (bingo call, clickety click) my upcoming birthday is hard to justify as a meaningful event, but time does on occasion change the rules. As a kid, twenty-one always had meaning but nowadays less so. Moving into my ballpark I think sixty-four had meaning. It used to be the age of retirement and getting a pension. Even the Beatles sang about it. McCartney wrote it when he was only 14. Listening to the lyrics as a person who has passed that age is quite mortifying. Here are some extracts and you'll get my drift.

"Will you still be sending me a valentine, birthday greetings bottle of wine." – The answer is a resounding 'no.' Valentine? I think Kerryn last sent me one … er … let me think … never. I don't really drink wine either.

"When I get older losing my hair." – Not yet but it's nowhere near as thick as it was and now totally grey.

"Will you still need me will you still feed me" – I do most of the cooking in our house anyway, so at least this isn't a big risk.

"Doing the garden digging the weeds." – I bloody hate gardening.

"Grand children on your knee, Vera, Chuck and Dave." – Well, I've only got two, they are across the other side of the world and their names (Drake and Lyric) weren't proper names when the song was written.

Now although this all sounds a bit depressing; I have to say I did have a big party on my sixtieth and it was a humdinger.

By telling you about the 60th I have contravened the most basic rule in diary writing in that it is out of the time sequence which admittedly is sort of the point of a diary. It's not as though I'm a couple of days out, more like six years adrift. I therefore need you to imagine that this diary day (one hundred and thirty-one in case you were not paying attention) is the same day but just happens to be six years earlier. I am sure you quickly got invested in time travel movies like

'Back to the future' so I'm sure you can for my diary.

Having booked the local rugby club, hired a DJ and a caterer (not the same person), the scene was set. The theme was a 'P' party in honour of the first letter of my name which determined the fancy dress code. Come as something that begins with the letter 'P.' I forgot to mention we also hired a bucking bronco but instead of a faux bull attached to the contraption, a comedy item was substituted in the shape of a six-foot penis. It was, after all, a 'P' party. Sixty guests were invited, it seemed an appropriate number, and not only did everyone turn up but their costume efforts were outstanding. I won't run down the whole list but here are a few examples as well as the inevitable police and prostitutes.

- ❖ Pandas (two, worn by a married couple which inflated)
- ❖ Pervert (two also, unrelated)
- ❖ Pocohontas
- ❖ Paddler (he brought along his kayak)
- ❖ Priscilla (Queen of the Desert)
- ❖ Priest
- ❖ Pilot
- ❖ Prisoner
- ❖ Popeye

- ❖ Paper Clip
- ❖ Pappa Smurf
- ❖ Pippa Longstocking
- ❖ Penguin
- ❖ Pirate
- ❖ Plug and socket.
- ❖ Pterodactyl (the resident intellectual playing on the silent 'p')
- ❖ Po (Tellytubby)
- ❖ Painting (a local artistic friend came as the Mona Lisa but eventually got tired carrying the frame around her through which she poked her head)

Jake was twelve at the time and turned up in a West Coast Eagles kit. He came as a Premiership player as they won the Grand Final that year much to the annoyance of Kerryn whose beloved Collingwood were the team they beat in the final. His grandfather, who came as Press Photographer, did a sterling job taking pictures to commemorate the event. Although he was less impressed by the sight of his twelve-year-old grandson riding a six-foot penis.

Dave came as a policeman which caused some consternation in the car park with a couple of local churchgoers who were concerned that they had parked illegally. The church, Our Lady of

Grace, is situated near the rugby club. But Dave's effort caused nowhere near as much perturbation with the local bible toting community as the antics of two other friends, Murray and Jeanice Krakouer. They were also strangers to the area and accidentally went into the church hall thinking that was the venue of the party. The local Catholics went into shock when a professor (full mortar board and gown) and a Pink Lady (Grease) rocked up unannounced. If the costumes caught them off guard, they certainly had never seen aboriginal people enter their little piece of Caucasian heaven.

The night was long, the drink flowed, and the party was a success. Some guests travelled across Australia and others across the world for which I was grateful and touched.

DAY ONE HUNDRED AND THIRTY-SIX

Played my last game of the season today. It was against the top of the league, Murdoch University Melville FC (MUMFC). There are a couple of teams in the league with the description 'University' in their title but ironically most of the players had never been to any University, let alone the one in the name of club they are playing for.

Two life changing events will follow my seasonal retirement from playing. Well, I say histrionically, 'life changing,' more like temporary re-adjustments. It's my last game because my long-awaited shoulder operation is due. A few months ago, I had a CT scan of my painful right shoulder which revealed that the source of my agony was a full width muscle and tendon tear. The surgeon was as empathetic and encouraging as surgeons often are (sarcasm alert) and told me with great enthusiasm it was the worst he had seen for some years. He also advised me that the recovery and rehabilitation period is particularly long. Normally twelve months to achieve full function but in my case nearer eighteen. I enquired as to the cause of the injury because I could not relate to any one single catastrophic event, and he muttered something about old age and gradual deterioration.

‘You mentioned two events,” I hear you say. We now know about playing your last game due to the shoulder operation but what was the second?

It was my transition from player to full time management. Gary, the manager, was about to bugger off abroad for several months to eat his way around Europe and I was elevated from player/assistant coach to full time management. I had also been away for a three weeks previously and arrived back just as Gary departed. His handover consisted of “we’ve lost the last two out of three, good luck.” We were third in the league having been top prior to the two recent losses.

All was not lost; the game I played today was my first as player/sole manager and we drew against the top team. Now, as simply the manager, I faced twelve more league games, and we were still in the Cup competition. We were going for the double.

DAY ONE HUNDRED AND THIRTY-EIGHT

Had the shoulder operation yesterday and woke up in the early hours of the morning with this ungainly contraption strapped to my side. Looked across to find a strange man sleeping in an adjoining bed. Given the small size of the room, the proximity was far closer than I felt comfortable with. I'd not even been introduced for God's sake. Apparently paying extortionate amounts of private medical insurance does not guarantee a private room in a private hospital.

So, I found myself spending the night with a new mate who also just had a shoulder operation. Let's for the sake of privacy call him Arthur. That wasn't his name. As it turned out we got on like a house on fire. Arthur is about ten years younger than me and loves football so our short time together was not as painful as it could potentially have been. Our time together would be limited as we were both just there overnight so the surgeon could check everything was hunky dory post op.

The surgeon saw Arthur first and being only a couple of yards away I was party to the conversation. Once he had finished the consultation, the surgeon patted Arthur on his good shoulder with the assurance that he would be out of his sling in three days. When he turned to me the surgeon frowned. I got all the similar questions, but he concluded, not even patting me on my good shoulder, that he would see me in six weeks at which point he expected I could ditch the sling. Like a child I protested that it wasn't fair and, pointing to my new best mate added, 'it's not fair doctor, how come he only has to have it on for three days?'

He gave me the look of a benign sage talking to his two-year-old grandson. "Because, Mister Coates, he had only relatively minor damage compared to your full width tear." This I assumed was a nice way of saying everything, in my case, was buggered. I looked over to Arthur who was smiling smugly as if he had won first prize in the lottery of crippled old blokes.

I left the hospital with my new addition (the sling not Arthur) which was, theoretically, to spend every waking and sleeping hour in my company for the foreseeable future. We are not, for the uninitiated, taking about a non-invasive piece of soft material here. This was a bulky piece equipment with straps and a sort of large buffer pad to keep the arm in a certain position. The thought of trying to sleep with this filled me with dread.

I returned home to find Kerryn had set up the spare bedroom which she told me would be my new sleeping quarters for the next month and a half. There was no way she was going to be disturbed. In the event, Alfie demonstrated far more sympathy which wasn't that difficult. His mild form of canine protest on my behalf came in the shape of his decision also to abandon the marital boudoir (not that Kerryn and I are married) and join me in the spare room for six weeks. We boys must stick together. Alfie gave me a tentative wag when I expressed my gratitude and led me barking to the scullery where his treats are kept. The love and loyalty of man's (the expression doesn't say 'woman's, you notice) best friend comes at a price.

DAY ONE HUNDRED AND THIRTY-NINE

First night in the sling is finally over. With two hours sleep, maximum, broken down into four half hour sessions, it was the longest night I had ever experienced. It's going to be a long six weeks. Of course, the injured arm is my right arm, so it is going to be extra challenging. It reminds me of the old joke. I'd give my right arm to be ambidextrous.

I also need to get used to pulling together the Subiaco Shakers squad each week with the knowledge that my name will no longer appear on the players list until next season. Anyway, an opportunity to concentrate on full time management with my own private objective of helping the team win something in only its second year of its existence.

Luckily, if you can call it that, the beach volleyball season was over, so I wasn't missing out on that score. Befitting our age and skills levels, we finished third from bottom in the table. It was also 'curtains' for my short golfing career at least for nine months.

DAY ONE HUNDRED AND FORTY-THREE

Being physically incapacitated and consigned to a sling for six weeks allowed me much more time to think and reflect on our football campaign going forward. I was christened TOAG by the team which stood for The One-Armed Gaffer. First game as manager and non-player went well. Our opponents were Hammersley FC who we managed to beat one nil at home in the very first game of the season and now faced them on their own ground. Clearly the first game was close, and I remembered the opponents left the field sulkily that time issuing the threat that the return on their own ground would be a different story. Rumour around the league was that they had a very narrow pitch which they were used to, but opponents notoriously found difficult.

We were now on their home ground with its infamous thin pitch. Expecting a tough match and early onslaught, I set up the team in a conservative four-four-two formation. Frankly, this was a far simpler and traditional formation and therefore much easier for the old boys to understand than the previous more modern formation we adopted. We started well, scored twice, and appeared to be well in control until our keeper had a brain fade. A speculative through ball was about to be dealt with by our solid back four when a high pitch scream ripped through the air. “MINE, MINE, MINE,” called our keeper who ran out of his box like an intoxicated giraffe with an extra leg. He swung at and missed the ball completely allowing Hammersley’s surprised, but grateful, centre forward to roll the ball into the empty net. Half time 2-1 to the good guys but the game was now wide open.

The second half was eventful. Not least because an ambulance had parked near our side-line to attend to another old bloke in an adjoining game who had a heart attack. It is the masters league so whilst an event such as an ambulance on the ground may have caused an uproar in most cases, it is far more common at our age. We played on regardless until the officials decided the likelihood of injury from tripping over an unattended stretcher was too much of a risk to bear.

In the end the referee made us move pitches which worked to our advantage because it was more normal sized than the infamous narrow pitch which gave Hamersley the advantage against visitors. We walked off victors winning 6-2. It was now a draw against the top team and a win against the fourth team having played on the emaciated pitch of doom. Things were looking up and the two defeats are now behind us.

DAY ONE HUNDRED AND FORTY-FOUR

As the cliché goes, 'don't assume … it makes an ass of U and me." I had assumed that the days of the irritating estate agents were well and truly over. I had not had a leaflet for some while until, BOOOOM, there's a new sheriff in town and he is shooting from the hip. He looks marginally greasier than the others and, rumour has it, he doesn't play by the rules. A rumour around the suburb suggested that he is shortly due in court having been caught red-handed removing the signs of his competitors from houses they had up for sale. In one way he sounds like my sort of guy, and, for a moment, I thought if I ever do sell my house I might give him the job.

In contrast to the others, his leaflets were full testosterone loaded, go getting and aggressive. Let's call him Pushy Tosser Agency (PTA), changing his name, as usual, for legal purposes. He didn't go down the route of extolling the virtues and skills of his agency, his approach is far more direct. At the top of the leaflet there are two words in a large aggressive font. 'MOTIVATED BUYER.' He goes on to assure us his client is urgently (the word 'urgently' written in bold and underlined) looking to purchase his/her next property and if we would consider moving could we contact him urgently (this time neither bold nor underlined). The black and white leaflet goes on to ask a question, 'Can we mention your home as we may have a buyer?' You've got to admire the cheek of the man.

Now I am sure, like me, you spotted the nuance in that question. Up to the point it was posed, PTA was all gung ho. Let's do it, let's get it sorted. Remember he said it is 'urgent' which the Oxford English dictionary will tell you means it requires immediate action. Afterall, he appears to have a motivated buyer (most people looking to buy a house presumably are) and it is 'urgent.' Yet after all this macho bluster he slips in the word 'may.' Not I've Got a buyer but I 'MAY' have one. Not so cocky now is he. Seeds of doubt in his ability to deliver perhaps. I am guessing he has a very small penis.

Does this merit a response in my war against estate agents or do I let this one go. One to park for the time being and put in the 'to do' tray.

DAY ONE HUNDRED AND FORTY-FIVE

Growling on the balcony drew me to investigate the source of Alfie's latest angst. It wasn't, what the American Rappers term, a case of him losing his shit. There was no uncontrolled barking whilst he skids along the balcony spraying the glass barrier with canine spittle. It was a quieter, more measured warning to whoever was below. Once I joined him, I could see it was Mister Mutunga with a delivery. These had been less frequent in recent weeks. Looking up to the balcony Mister Mutunga gave a tentative wave and half smile to me. I reciprocated although the impact of my own bonhomie was mitigated by a warning growl from Alfie.

I feel he, Alfie not Mister Mutunga, has continued to improve on the racism front. Even white people, outside close friends and family get a low-level growl. I went downstairs and collected the parcel left at the gate as Mister Mutunga's van disappeared over the horizon. (Our street rises to a small hill in the middle and then drops off again).

After shaking the box and then reading the label, I was, as usual, none the wiser regarding the contents of Kerryn's latest purchase. I have no idea what she orders and even more perplexing where she stores it all. Occasionally she will accuse me of allowing dodgy items to be charged to my credit card to which I deny all knowledge. Just as I am about to call the bank to cancel the card due a suspected fraud, she tells me to leave it because she realises that it was something she ordered. Maybe she's a drug mule for a south American criminal cartel.

DAY ONE HUNDRED AND FORTY-SIX

More vociferous barking from the balcony drew me, once more, to investigate the source of Alfie's angst. I was expecting the interlopers at the gate to be of non-Caucasian ethnicity, but I was proved wrong. I looked down at the expectant pasty-faced pair who looked as though they needed a good meal and a healthy dose of vitamin D. However, they both wore black suits which may have been enough to make Alfie's hackles rise. With a good idea of who they were and what they wanted, I made my way downstairs with Alfie snapping at my heels determined to sort matters out.

Once I opened the door and allowed Alfie to approach the pair, he did his usual half-hearted rush, barking furiously. Their pasty faces achieved what I thought would be impossible, they turned even paler with fear. Satisfied with his work Alfie returned to the safety of my legs as I re-assured them that Alfie wasn't a biter, just a barker. I asked what I could do to help, although in truth it didn't take Sherlock Holmes to deduce the purpose of their visit.

They told me that the main reason for their visit was to tell me about God's Kingdom which they explained is the only hope for suffering mankind. I told them, pointing to my sling, that this bloody thing is insufferable and is it something God could sort out for me. They muttered something about God's will.

Now full disclosure here. I know very little about religion, it hasn't really held my interest the way food, music, football, and sport generally have. Not to mention my pursuit of the female form (further disclosure I am identifying as male heterosexual today) in the days when my body contained some testosterone. Those days are, of course, long gone. I say full disclosure, but this is only to you as the reader, not the awkward looking pasty blokes that were stood I front of me.

"Now gentlemen, what are you both? Morons or something?" They corrected me that it was Mormons, not morons, but no they weren't Mormons, they were in fact Jehovah's Witnesses.

Maintaining my obtuseness, I asked what Jehovah had been accused of that required him to produce witnesses. To my surprise he came back with an answer to counter my smart-arse question.

"We are called this because we can testify, just like a witness in court, about Jehovah and defend him because God is always slandered."

“Slandered? Sounds like he needs a good lawyer. Who’s this Jehovah and what’s he got to do with God?” I asked.

With an expression that was fifty percent patronising and fifty percent pitying, they told me that Jehovah was God’s personal name.

“Interesting,” I replied. “Presumably that means that God isn’t the most powerful being.”

They looked confused so I elucidated.

“So, if it is his given name then someone more senior, maybe God’s parents, gave it to him. Dare I ask, who christened God, Jehovah?”

They looked at me as if I didn’t have the mental capacity to tie my own shoelaces and gave me some explanation which I can’t recall and record in my diary. Put your answers, dear reader, on a postcard and send them to me.

In the event we had quite a nice chat and whilst there were some significant belief differences between us, we did have limited common ground. A couple of examples I can remember are that they don’t celebrate birthdays, which is true for me once I had passed sixty. I did, as you may recall, go out with a humdinger party. They had another rule about not allowing people of the same gender to pray in the same bedroom. I go one better, no-one of any gender prays in my bedroom. Of course we were significantly divergent on most issues such as sexuality, blood transfusions, and tattoos.

I didn't know that you weren't allowed to have a tattoo. Incredulous, I asked "what, not even if it was a cross?"

"Especially not a cross," came back the response. "We don't believe in the cross, we believe Jesus was executed on a stake."

I was beginning to find the conversation boring, not to mention I had an urgent need to pee, which happens more often these days, so I bid them "g'day" and off they trotted. I think they regarded their visit to me as relatively successful, unlike Alfie who had fallen asleep at my feet.

DAY ONE HUNDRED AND FIFTY

Had my monthly visit to Facebook today. I have an account but rarely have any, what I would regard as valid, reason to post anything. Of course, my standard of what is 'postable' is clearly well above what the majority regard as reasonable. Hence the plethora of posts of people sitting in restaurants photographing their dinner. But what winds me up the most is the person who posts the pearls of wisdom designed to show people how clever, empathetic, caring, wise or insightful they are. But if they were all those things then, surely, they would create their own pearls of wisdom as opposed to just googling and writing what some other genius came up with. Philosophising vicariously.

Today's puerile homily is 'if you wouldn't like it done to you, don't do it to others." Which is fine but not the universal truth it claims to be. If your mate is a masochist, he or she or they may totally disagree with this.

Then there are the prolific posters who try to project themselves as deep thinkers imbued with intellect, insight, and emotional intelligence by putting up clever quotes from famous people. It's a clumsy and lazy tool to claim intelligence by association. Worse still it's not always that clever or well thought through anyway. One keyboard guru put up Franklin D. Roosevelt's quote about nothing to fear but fear itself. Well, if you are in a plane which has lost all its engines then it isn't just fear you must fear but the impending collision with the nearest mountain.

Facebook is, I find, useful to get a feel for what is going on with more distant (geographically not emotionally) friends and relatives. Setting them aside you also get drawn into lots of other posts and it never ceases to surprise me what amazing, interesting lives people lead, all with perfect relationships and meaningful friendships. Everyone also has far more friends than me, but at least I've physically met mine. I doubt this is true of a large majority of younger people, with thousands of friends, who deign to leave themselves on this more archaic and clumsy social media tool. Most self-respecting youngsters wouldn't be seen dead on it and what is left is a mixture of the old, middle-aged, and desperate.

Now the process of taking Alfie for a walk takes longer and longer as he gets older. There is a lot more stopping off and sniffing at trees, signs and any other items which have been the target of a pissing dog. When he was a puppy, Alfie would be racing off in every direction unable to stand still, let alone spend five minutes sniffing a lamppost. Then, in a moment of clarity (an epiphany if you will) it struck me. Dogs pissing on items to leave their mark is their version of Facebook. They are not meeting each other face to face but they know who has been where and piss, rather than post on social media, to acknowledge that they have read the piss. If you see what I mean. I therefore encourage any dog owners not to drag them along impatiently but give them a moment. They are just reading their own Facebook and posting a response.

DAY ONE HUNDRED AND FIFTY-FOUR

You remember PTA (Pushy Tosser Agency) and his aggressive go-getting leaflet urging you to sell your house? As promised, I parked it for a while to consider whether I should act. Well today I did, under cover of darkness, having received a second identical leaflet. You'd think they would keep track of who they've posted stuff to, a shocking waste of money and duplicated effort in my book. It prompted me to hatch a plan so cunning that it would not kill two birds with one proverbial stone, but three.

Armed with the two leaflets, my son's electric scooter, and a tube of glue I set off an hour after sunset. Less a dawn raid more of a dusk raid. At the first house in an adjoining street, I saw a 'For Sale' sign put up by my old friends TAP (Timewasters, Annoying and Pointless). With impressive efficiency, if I say so myself, I took the first of my two leaflets from PTA and glued it to the sign. After pausing to admire my handy work, I then scooted off and eventually found another 'For Sale' sign. This one was erected by TAPs sworn enemies and fierce competitors, SAW (Smug and Worthless). The second leaflet was tactically glued to this sign over the image of

Smug's smiling smug face. Not smiling now, I chuckled to myself. I have found that maturity doesn't come with age. At least not in my case. An image of Worthless was next to Smug but escaped untouched because the leaflet wasn't big enough.

When I got home Kerryn asked me where I'd been, and I told her just for a scoot. She absent-mindedly commented that I looked very pleased with myself and I should scoot off more often. I was left unsure as to whether this was a genuine suggestion coming from a place of caring about my physical and mental health or something more sinister relating to her more deep-seated wishes for the future. Loose lips sink ships as they said on the World War Two propaganda posters. So, I kept my little escapade to myself.

Sometimes the problem with cunning plans is that you never really find out what, if any, is the fall-out of your endeavour. Still knowing how TAP and SAW went at each other last time I scribbled a little note on TAPs leaflets, I am hopeful that a new side will have entered the local estate agent war. Three birds with one stone. I'm a bloody genius. My favourite German, Mister Schadenfreude, was in the house.

DAY ONE HUNDRED AND FIFTY-EIGHT

With my arm freshly out of the sling, I went to a training session today and they decided to have a session of walking football. Whilst I am several months away from a fully functioning shoulder, I felt this was a safe activity. I say safe but I really meant shameful. It's a sobering statement about the point of life you have reached when you have been relegated to walking football. Despite the best intentions of those encouraging you in your advanced years, it provides no comfort when I am told by well-meaning (for well-meaning read patronising) younger people that I am doing well to be moving at all given my age.

I imagine walking football is a rare experience for most, but it did feel as though I was magically transported into a Benny Hill video. You know the ones. Those where the film is speeded up whilst the old pervert chases scantily clad young women to the tune of that saxophone classic, Yakety Sax. Throughout the game everybody tried to move fast in the confines of having to walk. They all looked like I do when I am at the airport and desperate for the toilet which is half a mile away down the far end of the Terminal. You can replicate the movement required to pursue an opponent in walking football by holding a grape between your butt cheeks and mincing around the house.

In the post training beer session – there is no better way to undo all the good work you've been doing for the last hour – Gary asked if we were up for going to see the Buzzcocks. For the uninitiated, they are a punk rock/pop band that's been going since my university days in the late 1970's. The band was founded by two blokes who changed their names. Although having the names Howard Trafford and Peter McNeish on their birth certificate they re-invented themselves to Howard Devoto and Pete Shelley. A very arty farty thing to do. A bit out of kilter with the aggressive nihilism of punk rock. Life often presents people who are one thing desperately trying to be another thing. This sort of enigma reminded me of my time at university where only a small percentage of the population proceeded to tertiary education and was mainly populated by upper and middle-class Herberts with a smattering of working class 'oiks' like me (courtesy of a now defunct government grant for those wallowing in poverty). I say this because there was a high proportion of far-left social worker party revolutionists who would disappear back to their country estates between terms.

DAY ONE HUNDRED AND SIXTY-TWO

Went to see the Buzzcocks, but it was more the Buzzcock, singular. The rest of the band had died, including the founder Mister Peter McNeish aka Pete Shelley. The remaining Buzzcock, Stephen Diggle, did a good job supported by three fresh faced musicians who could easily have been his children. Credit to Mister Diggle. Not bad for a sixty-nine-year-old. Obviously at my age when I go to see a band from my youth we are talking about blokes and women well past the state pension eligibility age. Still being alive is a minor miracle. Still able to give a creditable effort on stage with the energy required by the music style, even more so. It was also quite edifying to see a younger element in the crowd appreciating the music. Given the majority were fifty and sixty plus, there wasn't the pogo dancing, spitting and beer showering that I remember from my young days. My ears were ringing at the end. No wonder my hearing is increasingly deteriorating if I subjected myself to this in my teens and twenties.

I crawled into bed in the early hours of the morning feeling quite happy and invigorated after the trip down memory lane.

DAY ONE HUNDRED AND SIXTY-FOUR

I had two separate pervert incidences today. The first was whilst walking Alfie at the park during a community event. Loads of stalls, bouncy castles, music, face painting, and other assorted activities. Trotting along the periphery of the event, minding my own business, Alfie gets accosted by two minors. He looked up at me as if to say "really, do I have to do this?" I told him to sit. They pleaded with me to let them stroke Alfie, so I sat down had a little chat with them whilst they petted him. I filled the time asking the usual questions in this situation, such as 'do you have a doggie at home?' One of the little girls asked if Alfie could lick her face and I said I thought that was a bridge too far and your mummy might not approve. She was clearly confused wondering what bridge I was talking about when her mother approached the scene.

Having shot the sort of glance at me which indicated that she thought I had a long criminal record of child abduction, I tried to adopt a cheery innocent expression to defuse the situation. Pointing to Alfie, I explained that they asked to stroke him but, clearly, I came across as defensive. The girls implored their mother to allow them to stay a little longer and stroke the dog, but it wasn't to be. She took both girls by their hands and dragged them away protesting. My reward for my attempt at kindness was the mother shooting a final angry glance over her shoulder as she scuttled off. For his part, Alfie was clearly relieved to be allowed to continue his doggy Facebook activity unmolested, smelling dried piss around the park. For my part I had to skulk off placing some distance between the community event and me whilst bemoaning the fact that life is not fair. I had been falsely judged of a heinous crime.

Firstly, I should say, before recounting the second pervert event, that Perth is a very small parochial place compared to many cities. But let me continue.

Kerryn decided we should make a rare trip to the Perth city centre, and we found ourselves eventually in Myers (a well-known antipodean department store). Having followed her around like Alfie would follow me, she browsed and browsed and then browsed some more. Eventually she took an armful of clothes to try on. We headed for the fitting rooms and as she disappeared in, I turned to one of the shop assistants and asked, with what I thought was a jovial tone, where the 'man chair' was.

She was the stereotype Myers shop assistant. Mid-fifties, a slightly sour expression, bad hairdo, and a tad too much make-up that could have been applied with more care. I received the full Myer death scan. She looked me up and down and then asked me to explain myself. I tried to be disarming but a sword wielding, political, religious fanatic, terrorist would have been easier to disarm. Curtly, she asked for clarification, and I explained that my (now even more) lame joke was just a light-hearted enquiry as to where I could sit whilst my partner tried on her twenty items of clothing. She tutted, pointed to a lone chair that may as well have had the sign "sad old man waiting for his other half" on it and waltzed off.

Settling down into my seat I quickly realised that the chair was located right in the centre of the women's lingerie section and my eyes were level with, and one metre away from, the crotch of whatever a female mannequin hides underneath her lacy ensemble. A couple of women came near to examine the Basque section (what my mother, in her day, would have called a corset). I tried to avoid eye contact but could feel, real or imagined, their piercing disapproving glances. Thankfully, they disappeared and left me alone. Seeking refuge, I focussed my attention on the screen of my mobile phone.

Phone on silent, I was watching the highlights from the latest Leeds game, when two little voices piped up announcing 'look mummy there's the dog man." I raised my eyes and here began a classic encounter of non-verbal communication through the power of facial expression. The mother from the park served up an expression of reprehension emanating through ice cold eyes and a twisted mouth. Her icy stare then transformed into white-hot hatred oozing judgement. I returned serve with a pleading, and I must admit pathetic, 'I am innocent of all charges' expression. In turn she responded by surveying her surroundings to remind me I was sat amidst scantily clad mannequins and rows of women's underwear. And it wasn't the daily plain cotton tent-like underwear that Kerryn wears I can tell you. It was the underwear bought for the 'special' occasion. One of the little girls was about to ask where Alfie was but suffered minor whiplash as she was jerked away and dragged out of sight by her mother. A muted word was uttered from behind a hanging row of Balconette Bras that suspiciously sounded like 'pervert.' Once more I was alone surrounded by lace and an awkward silence until the Myers assistant's head popped around the suspender belts and shot me a raised, overly painted, eyebrow which seemed to communicate 'serves you right.'

Five minutes later, or should I say six minutes too late, Kerryn re-appears to announce that none of the twenty items were suitable.

DAY ONE HUNDRED AND SEVENTY-ONE

It was game day, and I was nicely settled into my managerial role having come to terms with the fact that I would not be playing again this season.

Harry and Tay, the Indonesian assassins, were sat on chairs by the side-line just as we kicked off for the second half. I looked back at them only to be greeted by a death stare from Harry. We had dominated the first half and missed a bagful of chances, so the game remained goalless. I changed the formation a little and decided to rest the two brothers with the intention of bringing them on for a final assault later in the second half. In the old man's league, you are allowed unlimited substitutions and players are allowed to go on and off at will.

With one of my disarming smiles (the sort that failed against the park lady) I enquired if everything was okay. Harry confirmed it wasn't.

By way of background, Harry is the team's MVP, that's not Most Valuable Player (although he is good) but Most Violent Player. A slight tendency to get involved in the occasional fracas with the opposition. So not the best player for the manager to have a robust conversation with. To keep our hopes of league glory alive we needed to win, and Harry expressed two concerns as he 'death stared" me. Concern number one was about my attitude. Obviously, I must work on my disarming smile which failed with both the park lady and Harry. He told me there was nothing to smile about. Concern number two related to my tactics. He clearly disagreed with my move to rest them expressing the firm view that he, and his brother, had presented the most threat and created the most chances.

Whilst I disagreed with the attitude point, I agreed that they had been playing well but I kept both thoughts to myself. There was a degree of petulance in my mood believing that I didn't need to explain myself, especially with the attitude I was receiving. But I did re-assure them of my intention to put them back on in twenty minutes. For the uninitiated, old blokes playing on a full pitch get knackered and bringing on fresh legs for the last quarter of a game makes a massive difference.

It remained nil-nil with barely thirty minutes remaining, and I could feel the virtual daggers prodding my back but chose not to look back around at the two brothers. I had brought on one of our mercurial Frenchmen, Gilles, and Back Door Binnie (nickname given due to a certain sexual proclivity he saw fit to mention during one alcohol filled session). We are a multi-cultural and inclusive team. Both had been rested for a long period in the first half.

Just as the imaginary knives pressing into my back were beginning to get uncomfortable, my silent prayer was answered. Gilles had a mazy dribble, starting from the opponent's corner flag he danced along their goal line, and slotted the ball into the net from what looked like an impossible angle. One may argue the keeper should have done better but we are talking over 55s Sunday league football here. I chose not to look back at the two brothers (as it may be interpreted as an "up yours") but cheered encouragement. Two minutes later lovely Gilles only went and scored a second. Vindication was complete but I chose not to verbalise my thoughts. As I had promised, I put the brothers back on, but the score remained at two-nil when the final whistle was blown.

When I got home Kerryn no longer had to ask if I was injured because, of course, I was now occupying a managerial position. Despite removal of my sling, I retained the name, TOAG (The One-Armed Gaffer). But she did ask me the score and gave what could have been a brief smile of approval at the continuing run of successful results. Equally it could have been wind as she is a vegetarian.

DAY ONE HUNDRED AND SEVENTY-TWO

Woke up to a very nice text from Harry. I have to say one of the most genuine apologies I have ever received – not that I've received many in my life. A true and genuine apology is a rare art. He said he has no idea of what he was thinking. In contrast I had a crystal-clear idea at the time and I'm glad he didn't turn his thoughts into action. Love was back in the air (to misquote the 1970's classic by John Paul Young) and I sent him a heart emoji in response.

Took Alfie for his morning walk and stood watching him for eight minutes whilst he went through his most annoying routine. It's to do with his modus operandi regarding the noble art of having a shit, or a 'poo' as the other dog people at the park call it. I get that it is a bodily function and gone are the days when you walk off, leaving the doggy deposit unattended. Picking it up isn't the issue for me. I am of course a great supporter of this societal development. It's more to do with how Alfie goes about his business. His pooing technique, whilst copied by many other dogs, is never matched in terms of elapsed time. It is not so much a bodily function but a ritual that transcends that of any other canine.

Commencement of the process is clearly signalled by a sudden alertness in expression. Staring into the distance, he focusses his concentration before he trots off with great purpose to a mysteriously chosen spot. Selection of the hallowed ground is, I guess, no big deal in terms of annoyance to the onlooker. In fact, this part of the exercise is relatively time efficient. It is the next stage which becomes a bigger deal. It's the spinning stage where he starts to pirouette on the spot for up to five minutes before he slowly draws to a halt. A final look around to make sure I am still watching him and then he does the business.

I have seen other dogs do it, but it involves a couple of spins, not fifty. Furthermore, the five minutes can turn into ten if he gets distracted by a dog, bird or any other thing, animal, vegetable, or mineral, which crosses his eyeline. It would be more tolerable if he would count the spins he had taken prior to the distraction as a valid, part completion of the ritual. But this doesn't seem to be the case. There are no thoughts along the lines of, "Right, I did thirty-two spins before that black labrador walked past me and I had to bark at him, I'll continue from there with my final eighteen." Not Alfie. He resets the clock and starts from zero.

In my continuing thirst for knowledge, I decided to google the phenomenon. It appears, that there is a multitude of credible theories as there are with all the great universal questions, such as the meaning of life. And one must admire the range and breadth of the theories that exist for such an esoteric activity. Some biological, some ancestral (from the wolf days), some hygiene related, some cosmic. Here are some examples.

- ❖ Spinning helps to stimulate the intestines (I must give it a go when I get constipation)
- ❖ Spinning helps flatten the grass to minimise the chances of soiling your fur.
- ❖ They are turning the full 360 degrees to scan for potential threats before settling into the vulnerable toilet position.

Many other reasons can be found on the internet, but none match the research resources devoted by German and Czech scientists. I'm sure the taxpayers of those countries would be thrilled to learn of how their deutschmarks (sorry Euro's now) and koruna were being put to good use. Setting aside what must be one of the most pointless pieces of research conducted, they came up with an answer which you can take or leave.

To maintain the mystery for a moment I must digress a little, although rest assured the digression is relevant to the animal poo topic. Now you may not know this interesting fact, but there is a plethora of useless animal poo research. My favourite being conducted by Victor Benno

Meyer-Rochow and Jozsef Gal of Bremen University (more Germans, no wonder they lost two world wars). These blokes decided to address the fundamental unanswered question of how much internal pressure penguins generate to have a shit. If I have piqued your interest, the work is entitled "Pressures produced when penguins pooh -calculations on avian defecation." Now I recognise that such esoteric subjects may not be your thing. If this is the case, I can cut to the chase.

SPOILER ALERT. If you want to do your own sourcing and reading of the research, then do not continue to the next paragraph where I reveal the earth-shattering conclusion but, instead, jump to the final one.

The Germans were able to calculate that these birds employed pressures of up to 60 kPa (kilopascal) to eject their bodily waste. If this leaves you none the wiser think about the effort required to play the trumpet. The average pressure that your lungs will exert when blowing into the trumpet is 7 kPa, which means at 60kPa, those fat little birds can generate a fair bit of power. Just don't walk behind them.

Anyway, back to the spinning dogs. The other Germans (and Czechs) concluded that dogs are calibrating and aligning their bladder and bowel movements to the earth's magnetic field. Yeah, right. They further concluded that they aim to relieve themselves in line with the north-south axis, not east west. They observed almost six thousand 'activities' which, I calculated, is the equivalent of watching an average dog do its business every day of its life. You can't say that my diary isn't educational. Forgive the double negative.

DAY ONE HUNDRED AND SEVENTY-THREE

By way of follow-up to the German's research and in pursuit of academic rigour, I took Alfie for a walk this morning armed with a compass. Whilst I, of course, have a good feel for general directions such as North, South, East and West, I thought it was appropriate to be as rigorous as the German researchers. The final data was thirty-eight full 360 spins plus one half, ending up facing due East.

North-South axis, my arse. If you forgive the pun.

DAY ONE HUNDRED AND SEVENTY-FOUR

Took Alfie for his midday constitutional having stubbornly refused to 'poo' during the morning walk. Almost immediately at arrival to the park he obliged. He faced West-South-West so clearly either the German's got it wrong, or their theory only holds for dogs with a German passport. Or maybe it's to do with the fact that we live in the southern hemisphere a bit like the water spinning down the plug the opposite way thing. Either way I think point proven and I promise not to mention Alfie's defecation habit again in this diary.

What was more of interest during this walk was that Superannuation man made an appearance once more. It was a classic battle between good and evil. The latter being in the form of a taxi driver.

I was approached by an elderly couple who were in some distress. It's funny how at the age of sixty-six I reference people as elderly but that's the way the human mind works and, as Einstein pointed out, everything is relative. Jake considers people in their thirties as elderly.

Anyway, back to Superannuation man. They turned out to be a multi-cultural couple. He was

Scottish and she was Vietnamese. He was concerned but calm, she was crying and told me she was not well. At the park where I walk Alfie there is a community hall which at that time was empty and closed. The had asked the Taxi driver to drop them off at North Beach Community centre and had been dropped here. They were confused and protested but the taxi driver insisted this was where they asked to be taken and had buggered off. It was a hot day; they had been wandering around for a while, and they were not in a good way. Some taxi drivers are cunts.

Enter Superannuation man and although I was not certain of the whereabouts of their intended destination, the Scottish gentleman assured me he would recognise it when he saw it. I put them into the back of my car, with Alfie on the front passenger giving them a look that indicated there was no way in this lifetime that they were going to have his seat. Luckily, my guess turned out to be correct and after a short drive they cheered up when their intended destination came into view. The man thanked me; his wife smiled for the first time and gave me a peck on the cheek. Alfie jumped out of his seat and escorted them to the front door of the centre.

Now I know what you are thinking. Superannuation man my arse. Always bigging himself up, making himself out to be the big bloody hero. In response I will quote a far greater and more talented writer than me.

“Always tell the truth. That way you don’t have to remember what you said.”

And to follow this up with a quote from Arthur Ashe that heroism is ‘remarkably sober, very undramatic.”

Now that sort of heroism involving no personal risk or injury, is my type of heroism.

DAY ONE HUNDRED AND SEVENTY-FIVE

Lesson, not so much learnt, but reminded today.

My neighbour at the back of my house had a bloke pruning the trees that created a barrier between our properties. Significant amounts of the pruning fell onto our side. My first thought was to go round and complain about the mess being created. However, when I went round to the neighbour's house, I found the pruner to be a young bloke who was clearly a hard worker and decided moaning wasn't the answer. So, I approached him with a smile holding out my hand (remember my body language skills – refer earlier entry). I introduced myself and he shook my hand. I explained what was happening and he smiled saying he had intended to go to my house and ask me if he could access my property to clear it up.

He came round, we cleared it onto his truck, and I gave him a few dollars as a thank you. Lovely human being.

The lesson. Try to be nice to people in the first instance even if they have pissed you off and don't assume they have pissed you off intentionally. Most people are decent.

Now that last statement does not apply to the president elect following the American election yesterday. Around 74 million citizens of that country think that an orange narcissistic, misogynistic, homophobic madman with thirty-four felony counts, two impeachments and six bankruptcies is the best person to have his finger on the nuclear button. Makes one wonder if democracy is a good thing.

I am slowly coming round to the idea that to be entitled to vote you need to pass some sort of intelligence and morality test. If you think I'm wrong, you probably think, like Trump, that;

- Immigrants will eat your pets.
- Wind farms cause cancer.
- Magnets don't work under water.
- The fictional serial killer Hannibal Lecter is a great and wonderful man.

DAY ONE HUNDRED AND SEVENTY-SIX

GPs, old people's ailments and old people, don't get me started.

In the vibrancy of my youth, I was always a little (how shall I put it?) intolerant of the older generation who would block up GP surgeries with regular visits. I had small children and when they got particularly ill with high temperatures and in distress, I would sit in a packed waiting room with my child crying and burning up. Around me would be a waiting army of geriatrics who didn't look that ill. It seemed, from my warped perspective, to be a sort of pensioner hobby to fill in their time with a weekly appointment to have a chat with the local quack. Once I did get in with the crying child that usually had passed out by that point, the result was predictable medicine (always the same anti-biotic) and the suggestion of a follow up appointment. More pain. When I attended the follow up visit a few days later I would sit amongst the inhabitants of the waiting room who looked startlingly familiar.

On a rare occasion where I required a personal visit and the doctor requested a blood test, I would go for the test outside work hours, typically a Saturday morning. Every time I walked through the doors on a Saturday morning to see the local vampire (phlebotomist) I would, once again, be presented with a full waiting room whose inhabitants looked startlingly familiar. Why did the pensioners feel the need to do this on a Saturday? They did not work and presumably had a fair bit of free time Monday to Friday. I even tried to outsmart them once by going five minutes before the clinic opened but they were far too clever for me and a queue of them would have formed in front of the door.

Once a sour looking receptionist unlocked the door, a senile stampede would run over her to gather the numbered tickets which determined your place in the queue. Short of bundling over a woman with a walking frame I decided to walk behind her and on my way to the desk. I stopped to help the trampled receptionist get to her feet. Harking back to my old Looney Tunes cartoon days, I imagined a series of footprints over her body and face. She returned my efforts to assist her not with gratitude but with a challenge. She enquired, very pointedly, as to what I was smiling at. I didn't say Roadrunner as I thought it was not worth trying to explain what was in my mind and muttered a passive 'sorry' whilst grabbing my ticket. By this time, I ended up at the end of the queue.

Now that I am no longer working, I am officially in the cohort I once despised. With the past in mind, I am determined not to be the queue blocker for adults with jobs and young children. I will not be having my blood tests, scans, or GP appointments on Saturdays, and I now endeavour not to arrange an appointment for every ailment or condition. This is fine but I am finding that I wake up most mornings with some form of ache, pain, bodily growth which, if I addressed everything, I feel or find, I would have a weekly recurring slot at the witch doctor.

My tactic is to save them up and today was the time to cash the latest batch in. My GP is very good, and he is happy for me to come with multiple issues, unlike the previous one with a nazi receptionist who insisted the doctor would only look at one issue per visit. Today's three items were a painful thumb joint which stopped me opening jars (I'd left it for six months), a mysterious brown spot on my arm and an even more mysterious lump on the side of my leg near the knee joint.

Apparently, the thumb joint was easy, and a common problem and he referred me to an Occupational Therapist who specialises in this sort of thing. It's amazing what people specialise in, but I guess one of the main characteristics that distinguishes us from the rest of the animal kingdom is possession of an opposable thumb. The mysterious brown mark it seemed was not mysterious at all, although the label he gave it was mortifying. He called it a senile wart. As if old age isn't mortifying enough, they must call a small brown mark (that would be labelled as a freckle in my youth) a bloody wart! And a senile one at that.

The leg lump totally foxed him and it's off for an ultrasound, which I can assure you I will arrange during the working hours for those people still on the treadmill of work life.

DAY ONE HUNDRED AND EIGHTY-ONE

Despite my best efforts to teach PTA (Pushy Tosser Agency) a lesson by causing a three-way estate agents war – you may recall I posted his leaflet onto the 'For-sale' signs of the other two local pests - he is clearly a man who is not easily deterred from his primary objective. You've guessed it, I am now receiving leaflets telling me which houses he had sold in the last month. At the bottom of the leaflet, he also urged potential customers to come to him because he was honest and plain speaking. He guaranteed not to confuse us with legal and sales jargon.

I decided to pay a visit to his local office but only managed to get as far as a trainee who looked as though he was barely out of his nappies let alone school. According to the man child, Mister Tosser was out of the office, but the infant helpfully suggested I send an email. In his best non joined up writing, he scribbled the email address in large letters on a letterheaded compliment slip. I assume he thought I was blind as well as senile. It was fitting, if not serendipitous, that his error was a schoolboy error. Unwittingly he gave me his master's personal email rather than a general one.

Back home I fired up the laptop and my fingers hovered over the keyboard as I pondered the inference of his leaflet. Obviously spruiking the fact that he is plain speaking and did not want to confuse us with jargon, he clearly thought we, the general public, are illiterate morons who could barely string a sentence together in either the written or spoken word. This set the tone of my email in which I attempted to challenge this assumption.

This is the email I sent.

Dear Mister Tosser (no I did not use this name but reproduce his pseudonym for legal reasons).

I hope you do not find my correspondence congested with sesquipedalian verbiage.

Nor do I want to appear vexatious or querulous. Whilst your leaflet indicates house conveyancing is an esoteric enterprise with regulations that obfuscate the process, I would postulate that your contention is solipsistic and ineffable.

I would repudiate the proposition in your mellifluous leaflet that even we ordinary people find house conveyancing tenebrous and potentially pernicious.

I hope I do not come across as quixotic nor obstreperous, in the following request.

It is my heartfelt wish that the flow of your uninvited leaflets into my post box is not inexorable and that this lamentable invasion of my privacy desists.

Trusting you find my laconic correspondence perspicacious and equanimous.

Your sincerely,

Paul Coates

8 Beachton Street.

DAY ONE HUNDRED AND EIGHTY-TWO

Gave Kerryn as small surprise birthday get together, meeting a few friends at a bar. I will never be doing this again. Having a partner who is a control freak, which makes Hitler look like the King of Delegated Management, makes arranging anything as a surprise, not impossible, but mentally challenging. Two weeks ago, I told her not to book anything on this day because I had booked a restaurant with just Jake, her, and myself so we could have a nice meal on her birthday. (Following the requirement that she did not want a fuss and preferred not to do anything for her birthday).

I got her to accept this unusual situation where she had not made the arrangements, did not know where I had booked and thus had no control over the situation. Worse still, she had no confidence of the person who had taken control. That person being me. I endured two weeks of daily whinging and when she woke up today, she asked if I could cancel it.

Bearing in mind the fact that getting the six friends together on an agreed date at relatively short (two weeks) notice was a minor miracle, I told her to suck it up. I re-iterated that it was just the three of us for an early dinner and Jake was looking forward to it. This was all of course a load of bollocks. I was using Jake as a diversion because she would never imagine we would be meeting friends if Jake was coming to dinner. He is a good kid but let's face it, at age eighteen on a weekend he had only one thing on his mind. And it wasn't dinner with his mother and senile father.

Long story short. We walked in, the friends were waiting with drinks, presents and balloons and Jake stayed for a short while then buggered off as agreed. A good night had by all and for only the second time in our relationship, I managed to give her a surprise party. She muttered "thanks for a nice birthday" before she passed out and started snoring. This short, muttered phrase is the congratulatory and appreciative equivalent of me telling the Pope that I had discovered the Ark of the Covenant.

It is highly unlikely I will ever attempt this feat again.

DAY ONE HUNDRED AND EIGHTY-EIGHT

Hooting of the car horn brought Alfie to the balcony barking territorially. Dave was picking me up to go to golf. It was time to test the shoulder but, on the surgeon's advice, taking it easy. Smooth half strokes not full bloodied swings. We also picked up Nick. Three men in a car (as opposed to a boat aka Jerome K, Jerome) set off for Wanneroo public golf course. I had not played for seven months so had no great expectations. It was to be more of an experiment to see how everything held up rather than a trial for the USA PGA tournament.

During my absence much had happened amongst the group. Politics had prevailed and Nick had resigned from organising due to his frustration over 'no-shows' and fee collection protocols. Furthermore, a full-blown refurbishment of our local course had put it out of action for a couple of months. Nick, who rarely left the suburb and stoically refused to bestow his patronage elsewhere decided he would break the habit of a recent lifetime.

Nick asked Dave if he knew the way. I asked Dave if he knew the way. Despite what appeared to be a very circuitous route, Dave responded in the affirmative. Twenty minutes later he turned into a car park, and we all got out and started to unload our golf bags from the back of his car. I say 'car' but it was one of those massive seven-seater, four-wheel drive beasts.

Nick and I were deep in conversation when Dave turned into the carpark and the only thing I noticed out of the corner of my eye was a blue sign which had the word 'Wanneroo' in large white letters. I did not take in the remaining words on the sign. Irish Nick was in full flow and his accent required close attention if you were to understand his long-drawn-out story. After loading the bags onto our trollies, we set off only to be immediately confronted by twenty school children and an oldish female. Judging by her expression she was sucking on a lemon, and she protectively ushered them behind her before asking us what we thought we were doing.

Who the hell did she think she was and what the hell was she doing taking her class onto a public golf course. They could get hit and badly injured by a stray ball. I was about to deliver a smart-arse reply when the blue sign caught my eye. It read 'Wanneroo Primary School.'

Three old blokes facing a bunch of little kids felt like one of those pervert moments I have told you about previously. Perplexed, Dave was about to usher a reply which would have been far more polite than mine when I tapped him on the shoulder and pointed to the sign. Realisation dawned; we muttered apologies and scuttled back to the car before the teacher saw fit to call the Police. Dave had turned off one roundabout too early.

As for the game itself, it went very well. The other three, Les also joined us travelling separately to the course, played badly and I played surprisingly well. Having posted the best score of the day I thought that I'd discovered the secret of golf. Don't try to hit the ball too hard and swing smoothly. Of course, anyone who has played golf will know that a good round is subsequently replaced with three appalling ones. It's one of the most frustrating games in the world.

What was clear from my debut back into the fold was that nothing much had changed. Les's scoring was as inscrutable as Nick's conversation and Dave played his usual occasional brilliant shots interspersed with more frequent poor ones. The only thing different today was that Nick's legendary 'Frazelles' were somehow not working. (Reminder: A 'Frazelle' is a wayward shot, exclusively Nick's, which rather than disappearing deep into the bush, miraculously hits a tree or other object and bounces fortuitously back onto the fairway.)

The obvious question was whether he had been to church that morning. On the other hand, I was blessed with what was previously the sole privilege of Nick. And no. I had not been to church that morning. As you know, I don't do church and religion.

DAY ONE HUNDRED AND NINETY-ONE

Minding my own business at the shops today, I queued to pay at the counter with two younger people chatting behind me. When I say younger, I don't mean slightly younger I mean half a century younger. Although they were speaking English it was a foreign language. They looked over a girl who passed by and said, "she's cool AF.' Other things were 'dope,' 'gucci,' 'lit' and 'slay.' Everything changes in life and amongst the most frequent are language and fashion. This has prompted me to compare my thinking in the 1970's to my current thinking.

1970s	**Current**
Long hair	Longing for hair
8 Tracks	Cataracts
Acid Rock	Acid reflux
Rolling stones	Kidney stones
Disco	Costco
Whatever	Depends

Think know everything	Think know your name.
Going to a hip joint	Getting a new hip joint

DAY ONE HUNDRED AND NINETY-THREE

Mister Tosser had not replied to my email. So, I thought it was time for a follow-up.

Dear Mister Tosser (real name not used for legal reasons)

I realise Estate Agents come and go, and I don't want to be the cause of your defenestration. Nor do I want to appear difficult and contumacious. Nevertheless, I am beginning to find your lack of response to my reasonable request opprobrious. It is not my intention to be procrustean in respect of my desire to prevent you littering my post box with your ubiquitous leaflets.

I do not wish to fulminate unnecessarily but I hope my request proves fructuous.

Yours with the utmost obeisance,

Paul Coates

8 Beachton Street

This did the trick and Mister Tosser replied that if I stopped cluttering up his inbox with incomprehensible emails, he would agree to stop cluttering up my post box.

We had a covenant, or is it an indenture?

DAY ONE HUNDRED AND NINETY-FIVE

Graham my father-in-law (not mentioned him for a long time but he had his legs blown off in Vietnam) approached me the other day regarding a charity he works with. You may recall my diary entry (Day 92) about the quiz night for the charity called Wheelchairs for Kids. The Charity is seeking to review and modernise its governance and set up a re-invigorated Board. My father-in-law kindly put me forward for a position. I met some consultant for a coffee at a café where he "interviewed" me for a position. Being 'interviewed' for a position I hadn't applied for which was voluntary and unpaid seemed odd, especially when he was managing my expectations saying they had other high-quality candidates he was yet to speak with.

My inner voice was thinking *'Well knock yourself out mate. I'll try to get over my disappointment of not getting an unpaid role I didn't even apply for.'*

I was further underwhelmed by the fact the consultant couldn't find my CV that he insisted I send in prior to the meeting. But the deal breaker for me was when he asked me my age (I told him

I was 66) and he replied, “Good. If we select you, it will bring in some young blood.”

I never thought at the age of 66 I would be described as young. I hope, if I ever do sit on this Board, the venue is strategically placed near a funeral parlour. I suspect business could be booming.

DAY ONE HUNDRED AND NINETY-EIGHT

Brenda came round the other day. Dave had pre-warned me because he had already been on the receiving end of three hours of venting. She was looking for a new pair of ears to batter and I had been lined up. In truth, once I heard her story, it struck me as a classic case of bringing together two of my own bug bears. The first is the (lack of) service culture in Perth, it is appalling. The second is my ongoing struggle with the new impersonal world of shopping. Gone are the days of leaving the house, interacting with the community, browsing, examining goods physically and testing them out or trying them on. Nowadays, you view online, place an order, and pay (revealing all your personal bank details in the process). You then hope that what is delivered to your home reflects what you have seen on a screen and your credit card details haven't been hacked.

So, let's move on to Brenda's tale of woe which started with her browsing the internet for a bar stool. After exercising her due diligence, she decided to make a purchase. Noting there would be a delivery charge, she decided to ring the store, place her order by phone, and collect it herself.

That was her fatal error.

Off she set and ten minutes later pulled up in front of a furniture store. Despite the lack of other customers, the presence of Brenda made little impact on the two young assistants. They had more important matters than dealing with a customer and giggled whilst comparing pictures and text messages on their mobile phones. Despite being studiously ignored, Brenda held her patience until one of the assistants deigned to address her. The other one doggedly maintained her gaze on the screen of her phone without so much as a glance upwards to acknowledge Brenda's existence.

Brenda explained she had phoned in her order and was told the stool would be set aside for her. Her statement was reciprocated with a blank expression from the shop assistant. Enquiring as to whether there was a problem, Brenda's patience was beginning to dissipate rapidly, she was told they do not stock bar stools. This unwelcome news was delivered in a flat tone without even a hint of regret in the voice of the shop assistant who just stared back challengingly. Brenda snapped, abused both the assistants, and walked out of the store. As she turned to deliver a final barrage of expletives to the young women, who stood impassively at the door of the store to make sure she left without causing any damage, the signage above them caught her eye. Not believing what her eyes were telling her, she looked to the right and saw the adjoining store had the sign ‘Harvey-Norman’ emblazoned in large white letters on a dark blue background. She had entered the wrong store. Determined not to lose face she shouted over to the assistants with the announcement that she would take her business to Harvey Norman’s. This of course did not bother the two young women, who were paid a flat rate on a non-commission base. In fact, both had already turned their attention back to the screens on their phones.

Having entered the actual store where she had placed the order for the bar stool, Brenda looked forward to a far more fruitful customer focussed experience. And so it proved, at least for the first couple of minutes once she had the attention of the man at the payment desk. Swiping her credit card through his machine with a flourish, he handed Brenda the receipt before asking if she wanted the stool delivered or to take it with her now. Looking at her slim body with a degree of scepticism, he assured her (for ‘assured’ read ‘patronised’) it shouldn’t be too heavy. Once he had informed her of the delivery fee, which was a third of the price of the actual stool, Brenda told him she would take it now if he could be so kind as to get it for her. Brenda may have thought her frustrations were over, but they had barely begun.

With a deadpan expression the man explained that she would have to go over to their Balcatta warehouse which was only a short five-kilometre drive. This prompted a heated exchange where Brenda sought an explanation as to why he had not told her this in the first place and how the hell does she get to the Balcatta store. Her concern was not eased by a further revelation that the warehouse was quite hard to find because it is located at premises set back from the main road. Unhelpfully, he added that there is no obvious Harvey Norman sign that can be seen from the street. He suggested that she needed to take the side road to the left of the Adult Sex Shop which, incidentally, she could not miss because the sign is enormous and there is a large red heart at the front of the premises. Brenda's mood grew still darker when she asked for directions to the street in Balcatta and received the reply that she just needed to key it into her SAT NAV. The man was totally disinterested in her revelation that her car was an old model without a SAT NAV.

Following a series of wrong turns, she finally pulled up to the Adult Sex Shop, which, whilst you can criticise the unimaginative name and marketing, was at least easy to spot. Her arrival was greeted by a leer from a shady looking customer in the car park. He winked and she sped down the narrow drive at the side and finally reached the oasis of the Harvey Norman's warehouse. She never thought that she would be so grateful to see the familiar blue sign with large white letters.

Having endured another ten minutes of administration at the collection hatch, Brenda waited until a young man with a white complexion riddled with acne appeared and carried the box to the car. Brenda was grateful for his help but questioned if he had the right item as the box looked very flat. Unsure of what to do, the young man called for the foreman on his walkie-talkie. The foreman was on a fag break, so it was a few minutes before he arrived only to confirm that the item was correct. With a withering glance aimed at Brenda, who was after all only a woman, he explained that the stool had to be assembled, hence the pack was flat.

Brenda drove home in a frazzled state. When she struggled with the box into the living room, she found Dave sipping tea whilst watching Antiques Roadshow. Inevitably, he got the brunt of her angst.

But Fate had one final trump card to play. Dave never saw how much the old bloke's vase was worth, having been instructed to switch off the bloody TV and apply his handyman skills to the matter at hand. The assembly looked straightforward. You could count the number of main parts that make up a bar stool on one hand. However, the task remained uncompleted when Dave announced, whilst examining the assembly sheet, that one Flange nut and two Cap nuts were missing. Dave's reflexes at 72 are quite impressive and he just managed to duck sufficiently to avoid the projectile launched from Brenda's hand. Luckily, her water bottle was plastic so there was only a slight dent in the wall.

Throughout the story I nodded and murmured sympathetically at the appropriate moments – at least I hope they were the appropriate moments - all the time wondering how Leeds were going to perform in the game this evening. A win would take them to the top of the league on goal difference, so it was an important game. Brenda left to find another victim to hear her story. I presume Dave was in a car somewhere between their house and the hidden Harvey Norman warehouse in Balcatta. Given Brenda's impatience to have a fully functioning bar stool, I hope he didn't get distracted, for too long, in the Adult Sex Shop.

DAY ONE HUNDRED AND NINETY-NINE

Back on the golf course Dave gave me an update on the bar stool fiasco. His briefing was an intermittent process as we frequently found ourselves on opposite sides of the fairway with one of us usually hunting for the ball in woodland. To cut a long story short (it was long because of the infrequency that we came together, not due to the complexity of post fiasco events) Brenda has a fully functioning stool. On the seventh hole our drives followed a similar path both landing in the twilight zone between the fairway and surrounding trees and vegetation.

I found my ball quickly, but Dave was struggling so wandered over to help. He was beating bushes with his five iron. After a couple of minutes scrabbling around I saw this white dot on the edge of the fairway some six yards, ahead of where he thought his ball had landed. Bending down I examined the ball, without moving it (didn't want to contravene Golfing etiquette) and could see it had the label 'Top Flite' printed on it. I called over to him and the conversation underlined the fact we were retirees.

Me: "Dave, I've found a ball."

Dave: "Is it mine?"

Me: "I don't know. Is your ball white?" (FYI Les plays with an orange one)

Dave: "Yep."

Me: "What brand is your ball? Is it a 'Top Flite'?""

Dave: "No."

Me: "Are you sure?"

Dave: "Yes."

Me: "So it's definitely not a 'Top Flite' ball?"

Dave: "No."

I picked it up and slid it into my pocket. Four more minutes of searching did not produce Dave's lost ball, so he decided to take a drop. As he was doing this, I fished out the ball from my pocket telling him that, for once, I gained a ball instead of losing one. He looks at it and says, "that's my ball." I protested by clarifying that it can't be because it's a 'Top Flite' and he replied irritably "yes, it is my bloody ball."

Golfing for seniors 101.

DAY TWO HUNDRED AND ONE

Maybe it is just me, but I occasionally get embroiled in a titanic conflict with a hitherto unknown enemy whilst shopping in my local supermarket. Today I found myself in a mortal conflict with a follicle challenged corpulent gentleman. Or, in lay terms, a bald, fat, tosser. He was pushing a trolley laden with biscuits, cakes, chocolate, party bags of chips, frozen pizzas, and a case of Cola (diet). I am sure people buy diet Cola thinking that food science has revealed that this somehow counterbalances all the shit food and nullifies the calories consumed elsewhere.

Throughout the shop we had numerous encounters whereby he employed the usual tactics of a supermarket nemesis. Nothing original mind you, just the following:

- Placing his trolley behind me as I get an item off the shelf. Unaware of the proximity of his hell cart, I rap my shins on the metal cage when I turn around.

- Cutting across me with his trolley as I walk up the aisle.

- Reaching over me to grab an item, giving me a first-hand experience of his under-arm body odour.
- Shouting into his mobile phone less than a metre away from me, asking his wife (nurse?) at home, if she could check whether they had run out of Mars Bars.

It was a battle that I had well and truly lost until the Supermarket God of Queue Karma smiled upon me. I am normally the person who picks the wrong queue whereby the person(s) in front of me are either needy, senile, or stupid. They are the people who cannot make a simple transaction without drama. These dramas can include;

- Credit card not working.
- Items with a dodgy barcode that won't scan.
- Paying with cash by endlessly digging small value coins from a purse. Each time a coin is found the customer squints at it for a minute to determine its value.
- Standing still watching the cashier pack the bag, as opposed to doing it yourself.
- Fumbling deep into a handbag, which resembles a black hole, for a purse, but only once all items have been scanned and bagged by the cashier. As if the requirement to pay came as a big surprise.

- ❖ Distracting the cashier with banal conversation despite the fact there is a queue of twenty people waiting.
- ❖ Asking for a receipt (there is always, presumably, a high risk that they may want to return the frozen pizzas, carrots, or potatoes!!!)
- ❖ Just remembering that they wanted a packet of flags after already paying for the groceries, requiring the cashier to unlock the cabinet behind him/her.
- ❖ Then spending five minutes deciding with the cashier which brand of cigarettes they smoke.

But having lost the skirmishes in my odyssey around the food store, I made my battle-weary way to the cashiers and, five metres out, was presented with a choice. The Cashier on the left had three customers (one being served and two queuing) and the one on the right only had two customers. I headed right, only to be blocked by my nemesis who blindsided me and cut across my path with his trolley brimming with artery clogging food. He was in such a rush, determined to get in front of me, that a frozen pizza toppled off the summit of his mobile food mountain and onto the floor. He ignored this and parked in front of me whilst a do-gooder kindly picked up the fallen meat lovers pizza and handed it to him.

Unable to bear his odour and smug smile, I switched to the queue on the left. As soon as I joined that queue, the person being served paid and walked off. The race was on. Now we both had two customers in front of us and my nemesis looked across nervously, although his first customer was already passing items to the cashier. But there was hope, she was not a self-packer. Luckily, the first customer in my queue was one of my tribe. This glorious example of septuagenarian womanhood was a self-packer. What's more, with fewer items (septuagenarians eat less) she caught up with the customer in the nemesis' queue. By the time it came to make payment they were neck and neck. My nemesis looked across; the race was now even with each having one customer in front. Game on.

Then the Supermarket God of Queue Karma floated down and bestowed me with her heavenly merchandising glory. The person in front of me turned around and said she needed to get past me and leave the queue as she had forgotten an item. Hearing this, my nemesis looked across quizzically and he was greeted with my best, smuggest, smile. To my nemesis's dismay, I unloaded my basket and the music of scanned items beeping must have sounded like nails being run down a blackboard. With a customer in front of him, my nemesis was helpless.

But the God had not finished her work. Oh no, not by half she hadn't.

The person in the nemesis's queue, was not a self-packer. As my items beeped and glided towards me (I packed my own bag), my nemesis shuffled impatiently as his cashier slowly scanned then packed each item. It was a shuffle of resignation. It was a shuffle of defeat but worse was to come for my chubby friend.

After several failed attempts to scan the non-packer's box of washing powder, the nemesis' cashier made the move we all dread. He reached for his microphone to request assistance, asking for Kathy to please bring another box of FAB Fresh Blossom to aisle four. The barcode and number had been torn and was unreadable. The nemesis gave out the large 'tut' and by the time Kathy had appeared with the substitute box of FAB Fresh Blossom, I was leaving the store after thanking the cashier. I looked back and smiled as I took in the glorious scene whereby the cashier in the nemesis' aisle was reaching behind to unlock the cigarette cabinet. I left to the wonderful sound of the cashier's conversation with his customer. They were engaging in a laboured discussion regarding the merits of the different cigarette brands available. For once, that particular conversation was music to my ears.

DAY TWO HUNDRED AND THREE

Went for a casual game of golf today on the Claremont Par Three Course, accompanied by Dave and Alfie. I say casual because the clientele are not golf nuts, and the standard is suitably low to suit our game. There is a relaxed vibe about the place which has a nice café attached to the course and the game itself tends to be more of a walk and chat, interrupted by the occasional chip, rather than the US PGA. Alfie loves it. He wanders alongside us observing all the appropriate golfing etiquette. The staff in the café are dog lovers, so he always gets fussed over and is given treats before and after the round.

In front of us were two Asian men. The son was probably in his thirties and the father around our age. Behind us were a group of four lads who all went to the same school as Jake. One of them had just been drafted as a rookie in the local Aussie Rules football team, the Fremantle Dockers, and popped over to say hello.

Hopefully, I have painted a picture of a relaxed civilised venue and so it proved to be for the first eight holes. Progress had been even slower than usual due to the pair in front of us.

Whilst the son could clearly hit a ball well, the father's swings were hit and miss. A lot more missing than hitting.

We joined the Asian pair at the final ninth hole where they were about to tee off. Following etiquette, we retreated to a nearby bench and sat in silence with Alfie laid at my feet. It was at this point where my two companions broke the serenity and protocol.

Alfie was the first to transgress and uncharacteristically leapt up and sprinted across the tee as the son was about to drive off. He had spotted a small group of birds and decided it would be fun to scatter them. Once he achieved his objective he skulked back under the barrage of my loud reprimand. I apologised and the son smiled and took his shot. We watched the ball sail towards the green. An excellent shot.

The father then took his turn with significantly less success and the ball bobbled about ten yards beyond the tee. With Alfie sitting beside me feigning contriteness, it was my other companion's turn to pierce the serenity. For some inexplicable reason Dave decided to shout out "nice shot." Shooting an angry glance, the son responded defensively that it was the first game of golf his father had ever played. Dave stuttered and muttered an explanation to the effect that he was referring to the son's drive, not his father's, but the damage was done and off they walked, huffily.

Dave looked to me for support to back up his contention that he was talking about the son's shot. With a degree of scepticism, I suggested that next time he should make his comment immediately after the good shot had been played and not after the one that had been shanked.

As with many things in life, timing is crucial.

DAY TWO HUNDRED AND FOUR

Followed up our little Par 3 outing with the proper thing today. Nick joined Dave and me for a pleasant nine holes on a full-sized course. Not much of interest during the game, though Dave nearly killed a duck and lost a ball in the water.

It got much more interesting in the post-match drink session - Shandies only, we don't go mad. Sat opposite me, Dave seemed to be shuffling awkwardly and ducking slightly as if he was using me as some sort of human shield to avoid being seen and discovered by a bounty hunter. No doubt my quizzical expression was sufficient to prompt an explanation. Dave whispered to me to look behind but indicated it should be done surreptitiously. I complied and saw a tall, skinny bloke in his fifties with greying wavy shoulder length hair, munching through a sandwich. Once the sandwich muncher had left, Dave told me his story. I will refer to sandwich muncher as S&M (real name not used for legal reasons) which as you will soon learn is quite a felicitous nom de plume.

Eventually S&M wandered off to join his playing partner on the first tee and Dave could breathe easily. Leaning forward conspiratorially, as if S&M was still on the adjoining table, he told me his story.

It transpired that Dave knew S&M from his teaching days when they both taught economics to a bunch of teenagers at the same school. Over time, S&M had acquired a reputation for being a bit of a sexual adventurer. I asked how he could possibly know this, but he said that S&M was refreshingly (or embarrassingly) open about it.

He, Dave, was introduced by S&M into the sordid world of suburban sexual shenanigans during a lunchtime conversation at their school. They had both had suffered a challenging morning educating (or not) disinterested teenagers and were relaxing in the teacher's dining area. There was just the two of them sat at the table and the conversation was mundane until S&M piped up to talk about his latest acquisition. Nodding politely, Dave feigned interest whilst S&M espoused the joys of owning a sports car which, apparently, was silver. (Apologies to the readers who are avid rev-heads, but Dave couldn't remember what model of car it was).

When S&M asked Dave if he wanted to see a picture of the silver stallion, the reply was a polite "yes." The reality being that Dave could not be less interested, but ever the doyen of social etiquette, he tried to generate a facial expression that oozed enthusiasm.

After two minutes of extracting a mobile phone from his back pocket, tapping the screen, and issuing the occasional frustrated expletive, S&M finally dug out the image from his extensive electronic photo library. Proudly he held the phone towards Dave having turned the screen to face him. Peering and squinting to try to fully process the image in front of him, Dave's eyes finally sent the brain an image which he could interpret. The photo was taken from the front of the car. It was indeed a silver car, but the photographic composition offered much more. On the bonnet of the car S&M's wife was laid on her back wearing a mini skirt with her legs splayed in the air in a perfect V shape. It was clear from the picture that she had forgotten to put on any underwear that morning.

"Nice, eh?" asked S&M, leaving Dave in the ignominious position of attempting to interpret whether S&M was talking about the car or his wife's private parts. Of course, I had to ask what response he gave, and Dave described it as a non-committal nod. Apparently, at this point S&M followed up with supplementary question.

Beware the supplementary question dear reader. At this point I must digress for a short while to explain the art and danger of the supplementary question. It is always a trap.

Now I have worked in roles where I have learnt to be wary of the supplementary question but value the art. In fact, in one role I presented value for money reports to Parliament, specifically the Public Accounts Committee. We would review a particular topic and make recommendations enabling the Committee to hold the Minister and Government departments to account for bureaucratic inefficiencies or blunders. This job required me to provide the Committee members with telling questions based on the findings and over time I became a master of the supplementary. Committee members were required to submit questions requiring detailed facts in advance, so the art was to construct a question which delved into the issue at hand by gliding naturally to an unforeseen supplementary designed to cause maximum embarrassment. For example:

Question: Could the Minister for Health please tell the Committee the total hectarage and value of land owned and managed by the National Health Service.

Various departmental bureaucrats would have, prior to the meeting, cobbled together a raft of detailed statistics to "over answer" the question with the aim of absorbing the time available to the Committee. This information was only of passing interest to the Committee. Their driving motive was to embarrass the Minister and win the game of political point scoring to create headlines.

Hence the supplementary would be drafted to maximise the discomfort of the Minister under attack and, if possible, half the Cabinet. See below.

Supplementary Question: Could the Minister therefore explain why over 26% of these assets, worth over two billion pounds, are lying empty taking up unused land whilst we are amid a housing crisis at record levels. Has the Government developed a co-ordinated plan to resolve this appalling waste of land and resources?

Sorry, I digressed, but I wanted to demonstrate the power and danger of the supplementary question. Anyway, to recap, poor old Dave had been haplessly drawn into examining a picture of S&M's wife's 'front bottom' (a euphemism, back in the day, used by my sister-in-law when cleaning the soiled areas of her baby daughter). He was not expecting the supplementary which was as follows.

"Hey mate, would you like to see a picture of my wife's tits?"

This dastardly psychological ambush inevitably placed Dave in a moral quandary. Does he say 'yes' in an act of politeness to avoid hurting S&M's feelings with a refusal. If he does, has he been unfaithful to Brenda and in doing so hurt her feelings. Brenda would never know, of course, and so should not experience any hurt.

Afterall, during summer he (Dave) wanders down to the beach daily and most days a pair of breasts are on show from a sunbathing tourist apparently unconcerned about skin cancer. It was an iniquitous dilemma.

I don't know why, but the first reaction I had was to look down towards the first tee to stare at the man who was the subject of the story, as if it would provide some mystical enlightenment. A beam of light into the recesses of his perverted mind if you will. It was a fruitless exercise of course. All I could see was an old bloke with skinny legs who looked as though he could do with a haircut, a shave, another sandwich, and a good shower.

Anyway, I didn't mean to leave you hanging as I am sure, like me, you wondered if Dave took up the offer. On this topic Nick and I were left unclear. Initially, Dave said that S&M showed him a picture of the offending mammary glands but subsequently, later in the conversation, he claimed he had declined. You will, on this issue, be left to make up your own mind.

What I do know is that Dave went on to tell various other stories, one of which was that S&M called by his house unannounced, to ask if he could use their shower. For clarity, S&M is a keen surfer and Dave's house is across the road from Tom's, a popular surfing spot.

Dave told us he was out during this unscheduled ‘pop in,’ but Brenda was home, answered the door and agreed to his request.

I thought it was time for me to change the subject.

DAY TWO HUNDRED AND NINE

Have you ever been the recipient of a present where the giver gets as much benefit and enjoyment out of it as you. For my birthday Kerryn bought tickets to see a show by the celebrated American psychic John Edward. She was keen to go and clearly at my age the topic of what happens after one's mortal coil is snipped, takes on greater significance. She also knew that in my case, I had acquired an interest from childhood because my stepfather was a local psychic.

Unlike John Edward, my stepfather kept this ability relatively private although there was the occasional businessman who would call in for a 'sitting.' These 'sittings' involved my father going into a sort of trance where spirit guides would take over his body and talk to whoever was in the room. So, from the age of eight or nine I occasionally would have a chat with a native American Indian (called Thunder Rock) or a German solider (Rudi) or some other spirit.

These childhood psychic sessions were fascinating to me and at the time I took them at face value. Certainly, some of the things I was told came true, even if they sounded unlikely. For example, to be told at the age of eight I would eventually live in Australia may not seem much to you in today's jet-setting world, but we are talking about a kid in a very working-class family in the 1960's. I'd rarely left the confines of the boundary of Scarborough, North Yorkshire (we didn't do holidays) let alone travel to the other side of the world. Yet here I am, living in Western Australia with, ironically, a neighbouring suburb called Scarborough.

Whatever John Edward does, I think he is good at it. Magician, psychologist, showman, psychic, I'm not sure but from my humble start as an accepting child I try to keep an open mind. However, many questions remain, and I did seek answers, unsuccessfully, from my stepfather to some of those questions. If he knew the answer he was unwilling to share it with me.

Without writing a whole book on it, here is just one train of thought based on what I call my numbers conundrum. If bodies are time limited but occupied by eternally surviving spirits who travel to an afterlife when the body dies, then how does this add up. In 1800 the world population was about a billion and now we have eight times that number. This leads to the question, in 1800 what were the other seven billion spirits doing? Just hanging around in the afterlife waiting to occupy a body? Is there a finite number of spirits or are these infinite? Does whichever God you believe in create a new spirit every time a new body is born? To me, it does not make sense or add up.

Now on to John Edward. Is he an exceptionally good "cold reader" where he throws out general questions, makes numerous statements and sees what sticks.

"I'm getting a P name. It could be you or a relative or friend. Who is this please?"

Three people put their hand up and John Edward picks one.

"Oh! Your uncle Peter just died. He's showing me something metal. What is this please?"

No response.

"Okay, maybe it is not you, what about the lady behind you, she had her hand up.?"

Excited to be chosen, the lady behind reveals information which the psychic repeats as if he gleaned it from the afterlife.

"Thank you, madam. To confirm this, your aunt Patricia had a small metal sculpture of a labrador on her mantelpiece which reminded her of her dog that passed away. Thankyou. She tells me she is watching over you."

Audience applauds.

If I point vaguely to a group of twenty people in an audience, I have a good chance of a hit. If anything sticks, I acknowledge the "hit" and move on. If I move fast enough, the audience usually only have time to acknowledge the hit because it resonates. They will not have enough time to process whether it is a "no" and then indicate this with a shake of the head.

A "hit' would often impact immediately, 'yes, I recognise this.' A 'miss' would have to be thought about and processed before a response. Can I think of anyone whose name has a "P" and what could be metal that John Edward is referring to. A gold ring, a silver necklace, a watch, a bicycle?

It takes an audience member time to consider the information, search the memory banks and decide that a statement does not apply. It is a lot quicker to respond if the psychic has hit the nail on the head.

Setting aside cold reading, does he use also 'warm reading" techniques with known psychological principles that apply to most people. Many grieving people wear a piece of jewellery that has a connection to a loved one. So, this can be thrown out to the audience in the knowledge that many people who attend the shows may have lost someone close.

There is of course "hot reading" where information on the subject is obtained ahead of time. This can be obtained by (assistants? Microphone?) listening in to conversations prior to a show, researching information if the guests on the show are known or even having a couple of assistants planted in the audience to get things going.

Kerryn enjoyed the show, as did I, but got angry when I discussed these theories and techniques with friends because she was initially convinced that John Edward was genuine. I retain an open mind. There are many techniques and explanations as to how John Edward does what he does with the motive of making money. But what motive would my stepfather have with an impressionable child. Maybe as a one-off joke to tease me, but not over several years. Perhaps my stepfather, not the most pleasant person, had a psychological condition or even split personality syndrome to explain the multiple spirit guides. Hearing voices is a recognised mental health condition. Three quarters of people with schizophrenia experience auditory hallucinations.

Lots of questions but no answers.

DAY TWO HUNDRED AND TWELVE

My career in Sunday league management has gone well over the last few weeks and our unbeaten run has continued. The latest game against Joondalup today was an exercise in snatching defeat from the jaws of victory.

I did say 'unbeaten' run, so what's with the 'defeat' comment. Well, it felt like a defeat. Joondalup always have a bit of attitude, and the games against them can get feisty, as did this one. Early in the second half they had a player sent off for what can euphemistically be called a 'robust' challenge in which the ball was missed entirely unlike poor Gilles's leg. It put one of our better players out of commission for a few minutes, but it meant when he did come back onto the field of play, we could make the most of our one-man advantage. We took the lead, and it was two-one with twenty minutes to play.

At that point they played out of their skins and if I did not know better, I would have said they had the extra player advantage. The inevitable happened and they equalised near the end. At the death we had a golden chance which was not converted. We had drawn against a good team on their ground which is a result we would have taken if offered prior to the game, but it felt like a defeat.

To have chance of winning the league the current leaders needed to drop points, but they were holding firm. They won, so it was all about turning our attention to the next game which was the semi-final of the Cup against MUM FC who were second in the league a point above us.

DAY TWO HUNDRED AND FOURTEEN

I awoke today to a chorus of activity outside. It came from all angles. Behind us Stan was busy dragging a steel drum along the ground and rolled it into his garage. I have no idea what was inside the drum. Could have been a dead body for all I know. Next door Erin was practicing again for a friend's birthday gig, despite her ongoing threat of retirement. Her rendition of a Sinatra classic was being partially drowned out by the sound of an industrial vacuum cleaner on their driveway. Bernie always booked tradesmen (car detailers, gardeners, and anyone else who could make a bit of noise) first thing in the morning. Our other neighbour's kids were out early, bouncing a basketball and shooting hoops. Two doors down Dave had his lawn edge trimmer operating to round off the morning concert.

To be brutally honest, thanks to Alfie, we did not have the moral high ground in terms of keeping the early morning peace. His contribution was to bark from the balcony at anyone passing by. When the intensity of his vocalisation increased, I surmised, correctly, that his long-standing adversary Mister Mutunga, was placing an early delivery at the front door. Kerryn had been working overtime on her online

Christmas shopping. She does her festive purchasing in advance, well in advance.

I waved to Mister Mutunga from the balcony, and he responded with a thumbs up, whilst Alfie barked. I think the canine racism had finally been dealt with, at least as far as Mister Mutunga was concerned, because Alfie's bark was accompanied by a vigorous tail wag. Less a case of familiarity breeding contempt more one of mutual respect with a healthy dose of entente cordiale.

As usual I toyed with the idea of opening the mysterious package delivered by Mister Mutunga and ordered by Kerryn but quickly dismissed it on the basis that I valued my life.

DAY TWO HUNDRED AND NINETEEN

The day of the semi-final arrived, and we were playing the form team in the league, MUM FC who were top of the league at that point even if they had played an extra game. They trotted onto the pitch with a palpable air of confidence, and I have to say if two or three of their players genuinely qualified for the over 55's tournament, they must have lived a very virtuous life. It was an evening game and, unusually, raining. Some of these players looked as though they should be at doing their school homework as opposed our lot who would normally be falling asleep on the sofa with a half empty cup of cocoa going cold on the coffee table.

I would be a little untruthful if I said I was overwhelmed with confidence and this looked to be justified when they took the lead early in the game and dominated the remainder of the first half. Disaster struck, not for us but for MUM FC. Out of nowhere, when the half time whistle beckoned, their central defender dawdled towards a soft pass from their goalkeeper. They were clearly suffering from a severe case of over-confidence and Jason, one of our younger players (in other words below the age of sixty), sprang from nowhere to dis-possess the defender and slot the ball home. I found myself giving a brief half time talk in the unlikely circumstances of the score being level. I invited others to speak and give their views; at our age there are no boundaries and frankly there is little that can be said that they have not heard a million times before. My parting comment, 'you've got this lads" was a bare faced lie and flew in the face of the evidence of the first half.

Surprisingly, we started well and applied our fair share of pressure in contrast to our first half showing. Twenty-five minutes into the second half we had a corner. The ball floated into their penalty area, but everyone missed the ball, and it dropped tamely to the ground. This precipitated a flurry of aged legs desperate to get a decisive touch. A game of geriatric pinball ensued as players stabbed at the ball to either clear it or, in our case, score. This seemed to go on for an interminable length of time until our central defender eventually stuck his foot out and it ended up in the back of their net. There was no-one more surprised than me, but I tried to disguise it with a shout of "well deserved lads."

What followed in the final twenty minutes was stressful and I was transported into my own managerial hell. The game transformed into a desperate rearguard action as MUMFC wrought chaos and vengeance. The historians amongst you will know of famous battles against the odds. Having more than our fair share of POMs in the team, Dunkirk came to mind where Winston Churchill conducted "Operation Dynamo" and sent all manner of water transport, military and civilian, across the channel to rescue some 300,000 men from being slaughtered on the beaches. Going still further back in history, I thought of the battle of Agincourt where the hopelessly outnumbered, but tactically astute, English defeated the French on their home ground. It's hard enough to get a win away from home in any endeavour, sporting or otherwise but the POMs did it and 6,000 French soldiers were killed, compared to 400 Englishmen.

Perhaps I over dramatise and digress too much, but they peppered our goal with shots firing just wide, some hitting the woodwork others battering the bodies of our gallant defenders. We had a couple of rare sorties towards their goal and got a free kick outside their area with five minutes to go. Our star free kick specialist chose this moment to take his worst free kick of the season, and the ball ballooned high and wide past the goal, over a small fence and onto an adjoining pitch.

Was I angry?

No, I wasn't.

I had spent the last ten minutes manically rotating players to soak up time. At our age there was no rule limiting the number of substitutions and, unlike proper football, players are allowed to go off and come back on. So, when Jerome, our mercurial Frenchman, ballooned his free kick it half a mile past their goal it ate up valuable time. Especially as their now fatigued central defender had to go and collect the ball. We couldn't even be blamed for time wasting.

When the referee finally blew his whistle, I almost passed out and was seriously considering returning to the world of work which, by memory, was far less stressful. There were raucous celebrations in the club bar afterwards.

We'd only gone and got into the final.

DAY TWO HUNDRED AND TWENTY-FIVE

Come the revolution, the first up against the wall will be all local authority councillors and administrators. Most of the hard-working labourers who must answer to them will escape the firing squad.

Along West Coast highway, the road in front of Dave's house (we are set about thirty yards further back as we look down the street at it) the Council has been conducting a review. The study had identified three areas where raised zebra crossings (they coyly called them Wombat crossings – fuck off) should be installed. Inevitably, the expensive study identified three spots along the four kilometre stretch which were pointless, but they nevertheless preceded to spend more money building the "wombat" crossings. Dave had been conducting his own campaign to get a crossing where it was most needed, namely the stretch of road in front of our houses. This part of the road is perfectly straight, as opposed to winding where the crossings had been put, and clearly a signal for the petrol head morons to put their foot down. If the road was a Grand Prix circuit (and some clearly think it is) then our stretch of road would be where Lewis Hamilton et al, would be allowed to use their DRS (that's

Drag Reduction System for the uninitiated) to enable overtaking.

Moving away from Formula 1 and slipping into cricket parlance, I had been called in to bat by Dave who felt he was losing the argument and the will to live. At our age, the latter feeling is particularly poignant. I wrote to Jobe Swearth (name changed for legal reasons as per usual) pointing out various issues to support Dave's campaign. Namely, speeding cars, pedestrians crossing to get to the beach, kid on electric scooters racing across with no road awareness … and so on.

I received the following.

Good Afternoon

Regarding an additional Wombat Crossing I can inform you that this project can only be implemented by the City's officers as approved by the Council. The scope of this project is to provide formal crossing facilities, and it is not a traffic calming scheme. Traffic calming measures and crossings can only be approved by Main Roads WA. The criterion for constructing a crossing is that the number of vehicles crossing that point exceeds 600 per hour.

As to matters such as excessive speed, noise from illegally modified vehicles and children under the age of 16 riding e-scooters, these are matters for enforcement by the Police.

I have attached links to the Council Minutes and Youtube where proceedings are televised and made available to the public.

Regards

Jobe Swearth

Road Safety Officer

Engineering services

City of Useless Dickheads (name changed for legal purposes).

DAY TWO HUNDRED AND TWENTY-SIX

As I suspect you have surmised, this response got my gander up. I clicked onto the Council Minutes which Mister Swearth attached and, for the literary buffs amongst you, it had to be challenging the word count for world's longest novel. For the record, the longest novel is Marcel Proust's 'In search of lost time' which is a strangely appropriate title when tramping through the bureaucratic mire of a local authority.

I also clicked on to the YouTube video link, but after fifteen minutes I gave up. There is only so long that a sane person can look at a still photo of the Council Chamber and listen to elevator music which accompanied a message that the video of the February proceedings would load soon.

Dear Mister Swearth,

Thank you for your email and having clicked on to the link provided for the February Minutes I am afraid that at my age there is probably insufficient life in my body to see me through reading the entirety of the script. The same applies to waiting to view the video of Council

proceedings which ultimately refused to work (possibly a metaphor for the Council itself).

Whilst I found your description of the duties of Main Roads WA and the Police force enlightening, I feel you have missed the point. It also seems that your interpretation of the duties of the Local Authority does have a degree of fluidity. On the one hand you say the crossings are the responsibility of Main Roads WA and on the other you talk of the Council approving the crossings. You also say the crossings are not traffic calming measures which I find perplexing. I hope and assume that cars will slow down and even stop at these crossings avoiding the daily slaughter of hundreds of residents. If so, the crossing must have the effect, intentionally or otherwise, of calming traffic.

Regarding the criteria of having at least 600 cars passing the spot per hour if my mental arithmetic is correct that equates to a car everything 6 seconds. I imagine only two roads would qualify for this, namely the Freeway in rush hour and the Formula 1 Street circuit for the Melbourne Grand Prix. Neither of these have, to my knowledge, a pedestrian crossing.

I note your job title is road safety officer and therefore would have thought that the sort of measure we are asking for falls neatly into your job description irrespective of the roles of Main Roads WA and the Police.

Regards
Paul Coates
West Coast Highway Race Steward

DAY TWO HUNDRED AND THIRTY

I was in the queue from hell yesterday at the local supermarket. The queues were long, probably because the holiday season is upon us. And Lo and Behold (a clue to the season) my queue had every type of shopper in it. If you don't know what I mean, let me explain and see if any of it is familiar to you. I have named them all.

Firstly, there is the one I call Charity Case. This person has queued for a long time but somehow is shocked to learn that the shopping process inevitably concludes with some form of payment. When the goods have been totalled up and the amount owing declared by the cashier, this shopper then realises that she must pay for the goods. Following a few seconds of processing this epiphany, she starts to scramble through her large bag handbag to locate her purse which is lost within her personal Black Hole. Why, oh why, didn't she have her card at the ready during the hour she has been waiting in the queue. This adds additional minutes to what has already been a long process but is doubly annoying when she is also a Princess (see below) and had nothing better to do in the interim.

The Princess is the shopper who stands motionless watching the cashier scan and then carefully pack each item. The Self-Aware shopper (a category I include myself in) would, seeing the long queue behind them, help to expedite matters by doing their own packing. Not the Princess. Add to this the first category and there is the third and deadly combination of the Charity Case Princess.

Then there is the Chatterbox who insists on travelling far beyond the required "how are you" pleasantries with the cashier. Ignoring the fact that the queue runs full circuit around the shop, the Chatterbox talks at and the flustered cashier often firing in a list of banal questions. The cashier attempts to multitask the scanning process, the packing process, and the answering of a hundred banal questions. I have lost count of the number of times I have heard a Chatterbox ask, "What time does your shift end?" and "Have you been busy?"

Then there is the Space Invader. Often males with body odour, who stand so close behind you so that you can feel the warmth of their fetid breath. I think their mentality is that the act of pushing up close to you will encourage you to speed up. They don't seem to realise that this does nothing to expedite the machinations of the Charity Case, The Princess, or the Princess Charity Case in front of you.

Particularly annoying is the Amnesiac Sprinter. You watch patiently as two hundred items purchased by the Amnesiac Sprinter beep over the scanner. Eventually, when you've almost lost the will to live, the last batch of items progress along the conveyor belt towards the till. There's a tunnel and I can see the light. A sudden exclamation of horror extinguishes that light. "OH! Dear me, I've forgotten the milk." Off the Amnesiac Sprinter goes, pushing past everyone in the queue, and disappears into the dark recesses of the store. Meanwhile, having scanned all the items and packed them, the Cashier smiles apologetically at the shuffling line of irritated queuers. Two minutes later, the breathless Amnesiac Sprinter pushes past the queue and returns with a carton of milk.

One of the most hated is the Passive Aggressive Pleader. You have all heard the phrase, "Excuse me, I'm in a bit of a hurry and I've only got a couple of items. Do you mind if I push in front of you?" You are then trapped, against your will, in a moral dilemma as the cashier and other queue members look at you expectantly as if a small child begging on the street has asked you for a crust. Now is it my fault that the Pleader has not managed his or her time well and is therefore in "a bit of a hurry." There is the assumption that the Pleader's time is more valuable than mine and because the Pleader clearly did not shop adequately at a previous visit, they find themselves in the 'two item' dilemma. Let's face it, the Supermarket is a place where one goes to buy a trolley full of consumables, and the person popping in for a couple of items does so at their own risk. There is no recognition that you have been queueing for a significant amount of time and have earned the right to your hard-earned place in the queue. I admit, with no little shame, that I have never had the moral fortitude to tell them to 'f**k off' and generally just meekly comply with their request. Maybe I will age to the point where I do not bow down to peer pressure in this scenario.

I clearly could write a book on this subject alone and, believe me, I have plenty more categories I could regale you with. However, I cannot bring closure to this issue without mentioning the Bumbling Indecisive. These empty-headed morons always appear in queues to food counters, whether it be a fast-food outlet, an ice cream parlour, or a bar. There is a queue, and it is moving slowly. The menu of available items is printed in large garish letters behind the service counter. It could, for example, be an ice cream parlour offering Vanilla, Choco Banana, Strawberry, Bubble Gum and a hundred other exotic flavours. You would think having been stood for twenty minutes shuffling up a slow-moving queue that you would have had ample time to scrutinise the offerings prior to ordering. "What would you like sir?" asks the server when the Bumbling Indecisive approaches the counter. Then the horror starts and there is an extended discussion between the Bumbling Indecisive and his/her friend regarding the relative merits of the Café Crème compared to the Burnt Caramel. And guess what, they simply can't decide and ask the server for their advice. The server may tell them that he thinks the Pina Colada flavour is very popular. They consider it but ask to taste test the Belgian Chocolate. A few 'mmm's later, they settle on Vanilla and Strawberry. Just as I relax now seconds away from placing my order, the server asks them if they want a tub, a waffle cone, an ordinary cone, or wafers. In my mind I scream into the dark abyss of infinity.

DAY TWO HUNDRED AND THIRTY-THREE

Had a little get together with the football team in a local hostelry. Everybody in good form but notably I had a first ever experience. Throughout my long life I have been approached by staff in such institutions with a variety of comments ranging from "what would you like to drink sir?" to "I think you've had enough and better leave" or something to that effect but perhaps less polite.

Once a friend of mine asked a female server if she lived in Bar Street. We were underage and his comment was only intended as a joke. Albeit a puerile one. She served behind a bar and a nearby street was called Bar Street – geddit. Yes, it wasn't funny but we were sixteen and it was the 1970s, an age where humour was less sophisticated. What we didn't know in our youthful innocence was that Bar Street had acquired the reputation as a favoured spot for local prostitutes to offer up their services. Therefore, the young woman serving behind the bar rightly took offence. Her response was more physical than verbal and my friend found himself the recipient of a beer shower. Having poured his pint, she decided he should wear it rather than drink it.

Unfortunately, my friend's response was to take my drink, which was poured first, and reciprocate the gesture. More unfortunately, the barman who was the size of an adult bear appeared from the hatch in the floor (he had been changing the barrel in the cellar) and witnessed my friend chucking beer over his colleague. His response was also physical, but he threw a punch instead of beer and my friend was ejected physically, with me skulking behind them trying to avoid a similar punishment. After my friend was launched into the street, I squeezed past the bear, who was stood in the doorway admiring his handy work. Having picked up my mate from off the pavement, we scuttled off into the dark cold winter night.

So, throughout my fifty-year career in hostelries around the world, my unexpected encounter with a bar server was a first when she approached our table as asked if we were the comedians. My reply, looking around the table at my teammates, was "well they are a bunch of clowns, but I don't think they are that funny." From a banter perspective it got a few laughs but whilst the humorous retort had not developed much in fifty years, at least it didn't get us thrown out of the pub. I looked around and saw a sign which indicated a space was reserved for the comedians, who were presumably a group of standup comics having their own Christmas get together.

Looking at their expressions it didn't exactly give off the vibe of a gathering which was a barrel of laughs. Presumably, ours did, hence the server's comment as she came to take our order.

DAY TWO HUNDRED AND THIRTY-FIVE

Re-acquainted with two old friends today. Firstly, Les re-joined the golfing group, having been absent for many weeks. His counting was as mercurial as ever and he ended up with the "winning" score. He didn't see the smirk on Nick's or Dave's face when he read out the result. However, in his absence, I had forgotten one of his other foibles which came to pass on the sixth hole.

We were playing smoothly without too much drama, consequently we were not holding up two very talented septuagenarian women behind us. Nick, Dave, and I preceded to the sixth tee safe in the knowledge that the two women were only teeing off at the hole we had just completed. Nick tee'd off, Dave tee'd off and then I did. We then looked around for Les who seemed to have disappeared leaving us perplexed and scratching our heads. Finally, we shouted out his name and a disembodied voice could be heard. Realisation dawned when Dave pointed to the brick structure which was a toilet. Les had decided to utilise the facilities mid round, as was his habit, and I am not talking about a quick pee.

Minutes passed, and eventually the ladies who had waited patiently gave a little cough by way of reminding us to get a bloody move on. Once the ignominy of allowing the ladies to play through was suffered, Les re-appeared, smiling at us whilst tightening the belt around his shorts. Whilst we are not slaves to every golfing protocol, we did request that, for once, he could do his morning ablutions and related activities prior to arriving on the golf course.

The second re-acquaintance, after a long absence, came in the guise of Superannuation man. This time my heroic endeavours involved another dog rescue albeit far less dangerous than the Monty experience. This happy little white fluffy thing joined Alfie and I at the park. After five minutes of playing with Alfie, I decided it was time to move on and looked around for an owner. I was a little surprised that he or she had not approached us sooner. But there was no-one to be seen. Luckily, there was a dog tag on the collar which indicated, as per the lyric to Bowie's classic track 'Drive-in Saturday,' his name was Buddy. There was a number to ring, but my mobile was at home. The only real danger present in this rescue was the drive home when Buddy decided to jump into my lap nearly causing a collision with the neighbour's car which was parked on the street. Arrived home, settled Alfie and Buddy on the balcony, and rang the owner. Ten minutes later the owner turned up with two relieved looking young boys and the rescue was complete. All in a day's work for Superannuation Man. Kerryn's only comment was in the form of a rhetorical question, along the lines of why is it that I always seem to get involved in a drama.

Natural talent, I guess.

DAY TWO HUNDRED AND THIRTY-EIGHT

The doorbell rang. Halloween is upon us.

Its origins are steeped in ancient culture with roots in the Celtic festival of Samhain, a pagan celebration to welcome the harvest at the end of summer. It heralds the darkness that comes with the winter months when, supposedly, the realms of the living and dead are closest. People would light bonfires and wear costumes to ward off ghosts. Christianity, as it tends to do, hijacked the concept and in medieval times the poor would go to the homes of the wealthy on Hallowtide and offer prayers in exchange for food and beer.

Now it's not only the Christians who can nick a good idea and turn it into something 'better' (irony alert). The commercially astute world of retail has transformed the whole thing into a festival of obscene sugar loaded greed. Whilst the Christians started the trend of exchanging a favour for something to eat, the commercial world turned it into a multi-billion-dollar business. Re-branded 'Trick or Treat,' we now have an industry rooted in modern American culture based on over consumption. It is now an enterprise which happily fosters greed within each successive generation of children who will, one day, be running the world. This is how that country ends up with leaders like Donald Trump.

With these thoughts in mind, I was stood at my front door and looked down at another two little tickers greedily digging into my bucket of offerings whilst a doting parent stood behind them with an indulgent smile. Whilst chocolate treats are being indiscriminately grasped from my ownership and transferred into their goody bags, I looked first at the excited avarice on their little faces and then at the contents of their overflowing goody bags. It's a portent for a diabetic future, riddled with tooth decay but, there again, it's not my problem. And off they skipped to exercise their infant extortion on the next victim without so much as a thank you. I couldn't help wondering, as I watched them race next door in their costumes, what a Unicorn and Elsa from Frozen had to do with Halloween. I obviously missed that memo but, looking back at the Celtic origins, I am not sure these costumes are going to ward off any ghosts.

Now I know that this all sounds a little miserable and sanctimonious, but I do appreciate that it is not the fault of the Unicorn or Elsa that the traditions have been entirely eradicated. However, the next visitors to my front door were taking the journey away from tradition to a distant place that was a bridge to far. I answered the door expecting to be presented with a Batman,

Spiderman, Snow White, Woody from Toy Story, Moanna, or the like. What I did get was four teenagers dressed in black, two from each gender (assuming they didn't identify otherwise) giving me the dead stare whilst chewing gum. The boy leaning against the door jamb managed to cobble together a sentence in between chewing his gum which sounded like "trick or treat."

In response I posed a question as to whether they thought that they may be a little old to be engaging in the practice of trick or treating. One of the girls muttered something which sounded like 'ageist old prick' but unfortunately my hearing had deteriorated enough to be uncertain. When I said 'pardon' her only response was to renew her chewing whilst staring at me in a bovine manner. The leader answered on her behalf, claiming that she said that they are not too old to be trick or treating as they were still at school. "Oh," I replied, "I assumed the cut-off point was post puberty, but perhaps you are all early developers." They stared, but there was no verbal response other than to repeat the demand for treats.

Altering my angle of attack, I said, "Well children, if you are serious trick or treaters shouldn't you all be in fancy dress." Then looking at the rather lackadaisical attempt at being Goths, I added, "there again, perhaps you are." The other boy, who was stood behind the leader, bristled. I guessed he must be the group's enforcer, and he took a step towards me, presumably attempting to intimidate. He returned my stare with a question which sounded more like a demand. "Well mister, are you gonna give us a treat or what?"

I had heard enough by this point and just wanted them to bugger off. Responding in a voice mimicking a presenter in a pre-school children's English TV series, I said, "Well young fella, would you like a little sherbet lolly or a nice yummy wummy chocolate bar."

Either ignoring or not perceiving the irony, it was hard to tell, the enforcer informed me that he favoured the chocolate option. So, I chucked them all a milky way each and slammed the door.

Trick or treat … my arse.

DAY TWO HUNDRED AND FORTY-SEVEN

It's the big day. The day of the Final and for the time of the year it is unseasonably warm. A run of thirteen unbeaten games preceded this, the last game of the season. We had finished second in the league falling a point short and it was either finishing in a blaze of glory or a muted round of back patting telling each other we'd had a very good season. I, for one, didn't want to be dual League and Cup runners up. What do they say about the runner up? The number one loser. Or in the words of Lucius Annaeus Seneca – a Roman philosopher geezer – "In war there is no prize for runners up." And judging by the last two games against them, the 'orrible Joondalup FC were going to give us a war with their usual menu of moaning, fouling, and verbally abusing all and sundry. Not to mention screaming like banshees when they get tackled.

Having had to cull our squad to the minimum sixteen allowed, five were unable to play but everybody was supportive. We had also lost three of our better players during the week. One had run a marathon a few days before (full respect) but his legs were now buggered. Another had an old man's disease, Shingles. The third has one of our typical age-related knee injuries.

Arrived at the Stadium. Yes, it was a proper stadium. Football West, the governing body, were going all out and a series of cup finals for all different age groups were being played through the day. Everyone arrived in dribs and drabs in contrast to Joondalup who came in a team bus. The mighty Subiaco Shakers gathered in the dressing room and, uncharacteristically, the day and occasion had made them quiet and possibly a little nervous. I did my bit setting out the team and structure and chatted to each and appointed Ken the captain.

We went on to an adjoining practice pitch to warm up and I selected the five penalty takers in the event of a draw. Not that this was a likely eventuality but better to be prepared. 'Orrible Joondalup warmed up on the practice pitch next to us. Eventually both teams returned to the changing rooms for a final briefing and then marched out onto the pitch - full premier league style - lead by the four officials in green shirts and black shorts. The pitch was pristine, a far cry from the Sunday league surfaces of variable quality that we'd played on all season.

As expected, 'orrible Joondalup started strong and frankly dominated most of the first half. Their goal had an air of inevitability about it. Now I know everyone moans about the officials but ... their fouling went unnoticed and unpunished whilst their uncharacteristically high-pitched screams when tackled gave them a bundle of free kicks. With seven minutes to half time one of our stars, Jimmy, broke through, rounded the keeper (the keeper was big lad and took a fair bit of rounding), and slotted home an equaliser. Arms aloft Jimmy milked the crowd and there was, to be fair, a bit of a crowd.

Half time team talk and back on the pitch. I continued with a constant round of rotations unlike 'orrible Joondalup who clearly wanted to keep their best players on the pitch. Now in my opinion this was an error and the heat, not to mention the age of players, began to take its toll. We started to dominate, had a goal disallowed for a highly questionable offside (the linesman was also flagging in the heat – pun intended). Said linesman was ten yards behind the play and couldn't possibly have called it either way but in the final analysis was influenced by the screaming protests of 'orrible Joondalup. We continued to press, and a shot from our mercurial French player, Gilles, travelled goal bound past the keeper but before it crossed the line Gary had a brain fade and smashed it in the net. This was totally unnecessary but gave the linesman an excuse to flag him for an offside. Second goal disallowed despite the protests lead by Gary. Our supporters, not to mention the players, were not happy with poor old Gary. This was exacerbated shortly afterwards by a slightly dubious penalty given to 'orrible Joondalup on one of their rare attacks.

With thirteen minutes remaining we were two one down. Now the number thirteen was clearly an omen and not just because it is regarded as an unlucky number. Thirteen years had passed since the club had won anything. But an omen is defined as a portent of good or evil and the question was, which was this to be? Poor Gary had his head in his hands.

Good or bad omen. A clue came with six minutes remaining. I had just put Jimmy back onto the pitch after a well-earned rest. We attacked constantly and the ball bobbled into their penalty area and was half cleared straight to Jimmy who was loitering on the edge. The keeper who had come off his goal-line to clear the ball was stranded and a sublime lob made it two all. Crowd erupted as Jimmy repeated his arms aloft celebration.

They don't do overtime at our age, medically speaking it is asking for trouble, so it was down to penalties. Five minutes passed until the officials got their act together. At least they couldn't give us an offside from the penalty spot, so all was not yet lost.

Jimmy scored the first then their star player, who had scored a penalty during normal time, walked up to take his. A little sledging from our keeper and the poor bastard ballooned the ball over the bar. One nil to the good guys. Up steps Jason, who plays for a younger team normally but just qualified age-wise for this competition (we are allowed four players between fifty and fifty-five). Usually mouthy and confident he steps up and shoots, or rather passes it back, directly to the keeper. A disaster. But the linesman flags because the keeper came well off his line before the kick. A reprieve. Jason retakes and repeats the same kick with the same outcome. What's that old saying credited to Einstein?

"Insanity is doing the same thing over and over again and expecting different results."

Jason had suffered a bout of insanity. We all know England's record in penalties. Having said that, 'orrible Joondalup were predominantly English as well. So, it wasn't all over …yet.

'Orrible Joondalup celebrate when they score the next penalty to even things up.

It remains this way for the subsequent penalties until the fifth penalty takers step up. Our man scores leaving 'orrible Joondalup to take the last one before we go into sudden death. The final penalty is scuffed but sends our keeper the wrong way and bobbles goalward. It's a cliché but it all seemed to me to happen in slow motion until the ball hits the post and bounces harmlessly to safety. No-one was quite sure what was happening (was that the last penalty?) until I ran onto the pitch towards our keeper to celebrate. Then everyone erupted and gave a collective roar of pure joy. We'd only gone and won the Cup.

We had re-written the Subiaco record books and so I re-wrote the chorus of the famous football anthem, 'Football's coming home.' It wasn't three lions (our logo is one lion) and it wasn't thirty years but thirteen. It wasn't Jules Rimet (the old World cup trophy) but it was the inaugural Masters Cup. But at that moment in time the joy of a bunch of old blokes was truly moving.

One Lion on our shirt

Masters Cup a gleaming

Thirteen years of hurt

Never stopped Gary dreaming

DAY TWO HUNDRED AND FORTY-EIGHT

Too old to drink the volume I drank the night before. Have the mother of all hangovers. Spent most of the day in bed. Never again.

DAY TWO HUNDRED AND FORTY-NINE

Tis the season to be jolly and deck the halls with holly and other festive stuff. Way too early in my opinion but, judging by the TV adverts, the season starts when Halloween has barely had time to sit down with a cup of tea and congratulate itself on another profitable year. Every bugger is full of joy and happy as Larry on the TV, but I am not sure that this spirit is replicated everywhere in real life. My expedition to the shops today proved otherwise and whoever Larry was and whatever made him happy, he was nowhere to be seen in the real world today. Goodwill, my arse.

Allow me to explain.

My day started as any other. I took Alfie for his walk. Although minding my own business in the local park, I was accosted by two kids who came running up to me asking if they could stroke Alfie. Listening intently to their revelation that Santa was in the neighbourhood and that they had given him their list of gift requirements, I couldn't shake the feeling that I had met these kids somewhere before. My feeling turned to horrific realisation that I had met them, and they belonged to the mother from hell who persisted with the theory that I was the local paedophile. (Refer much earlier in the diary). She dragged them away and muttered something which did not sound complimentary. Before she disappeared into the distance, I shouted 'Merry Christmas.' She gave me the finger.

I dropped off Alfie and headed to engage in some early festive purchasing to disprove the male stereotype that those of my gender do all their shopping on Christmas Eve. If that applied to me this year, I had started seven weeks early. Driving into the underground car park of the local shopping centre I noticed a woman reverse into a space and give the car behind a little nudge. By the time I had parked she had disappeared into the centre but had not left any note. She had left a sizeable dent in the front wheel arch of the car behind her. Goodwill to all men, I think not.

Inside the centre a festive Grotto had been created in the middle of the main concourse. An old bloke, sweating profusely and looking like he was going to pass out or expire permanently, was dressed as Santa. His body odour permeated the whole Grotto, and I feared for his life which was threatened by impending heat exhaustion. I presume the two kids of the devil mother had been customers earlier. I also presume that she felt it was okay for her little angels to sit on the lap of a stranger dressed in a dodgy costume who she knew was guilty of misrepresentation and making false promises. And she calls me the paedophile. Go figure.

In Kmart, always a melting pot full of the rich diversity of modern society, I witnessed a tag team wrestling contest. From what I could tell, two women had made a dash and grab for a toy on the top shelf, and both ended in a heap. Later I learnt that it was the last one of these toys in the store and it was a 'must have' for six-year-olds this season. Seeing the rather unseemly scramble for physical dominance, one of the husbands appeared and tried to drag one of the women off the other. The other being his wife. At that point, a teenager the size of a polar bear then attacked the husband in a desperate bid to save his mother. Eventually security was called, and once all parties were separated, it became evident that the remaining toy that caused an in-store war, was broken in the melee.

If I continue to regale you with other experiences during this expedition, then you will surely have me well and truly labelled as the Grinch. However, I cannot sign off this diary entry without relaying one particular endeavour which could be called Grinchesque, but in my mind was pure genius.

Christmas lights in the neighbourhood is a big thing, and the same people compete every year to set up a display outside their house which consumes enough electricity to run the national grid of a small African country. I drove past one particular house which, if not the best every year, is the runner-up. The whole house was covered with multi-coloured lights and electric stars and bells sparkled everywhere. A nativity scene adorned the centre of the garden and was tastefully back lit with faux candles. A light above baby Jesus flashed to emphasise his heavenly glory. Elsewhere a Santa was going down a large chimney, mechanical elves were working in a workshop, and a model of a reindeer moved its mouth mechanically apparently singing 'Rudolph the red nosed reindeer.' Frankly if you were to stare at the display for too long without sunglasses, you'd go blind.

Clearly the owner of the neighbouring house had given up trying to compete years ago and responded with one small sign. It was in the shape of an arrow and pointed to the display next door with one word written on the sign. That word was 'ditto.' Pure genius.

DAY TWO HUNDRED AND FIFTY

Jake came home from work today. On his non-Uni days, he earns cash working for a furniture company doing deliveries and unloading stock from sea containers into the warehouse. His grand uncle, Billy (brother-in-law to his grandfather), also does a few hours to earn a bit of extra cash to supplement his pension. During the conversation he did not reference Billy by his name but called him the Milkman. I asked the obvious question as to why he was calling Billy the Milkman, and he responded that this was the name given to him by the other workers. It transpired that Billy gets paid by the hour so whenever he is given a task, he 'milks' it to make it last longer than necessary and maximise his earnings.

Apparently, at least half of the workers there have acquired a nickname, and Jake took me through the names of his four team members. Foreskin is so called because when things get hard, he disappears. Mastercard always takes the credit for someone else's work. Blister only appears when the hard work is done. Finally, Sensor Light, my personal favourite, only starts working if someone walks past. It strikes me that amongst that lot, not a lot of work gets done and what is done takes a fair amount of time.

DAY TWO HUNDRED AND FIFTY-FOUR

Bin day tomorrow and I was, once more, stood outside my house debating with Dave one of the great dilemmas that the two of us face on a weekly basis. Is it the week for the Yellow (recyclable rubbish) bin or the Green (garden organics) bin. If your memory is superior to mine, then you will recall that this dilemma and discussion with Dave led me down the path of my university philosophy tutorials and Theseus' ship. The quandary and outcome of the current weekly challenge took me, once more, back to philosophical theories and principles. Nice to know my degree at an English university was useful for something but I would never have guessed it would be applied almost fifty years later to waste collection on the other side of the globe.

It was a balmy summer evening on our deserted street where the light of the day had surrendered to darkness which set the scene for the philosophical discussion. Dave and I debated whether we were going green or yellow this week but failed to arrive at a definitive answer. Predictably we reverted to the tried and not so successfully tested method of looking up the street to see what the other residents were doing.

We were presented with a sea of yellow. Clearly our half of the street was unanimous save one or two rogue interlopers, rebels if you will, who had gone green. Due to a slight raised brow in the middle of the road the bins of the residents on the eastern half of the street were not visible.

At the sight of the yellow bins Dave declared, with the air of absolute certainty, that it was yellow bin day. I, however, had a nagging doubt because somewhere in the recesses of my failing memory a lecture in our philosophy of science stream came forefront to my mind. It was a lecture delivered by a pompous and self-satisfied educator who was smugly drumming the principles of deductive and inductive reasoning into the heads of thirty confused students.

Dave had fallen into the trap of mistaking his reasoning as deductive, which is the foundation of Sherlock Holmes' logic, when his reasoning was, in fact, inductive. Without going into the excruciating detail of an hour's lecture I was tortured with in the late 1970's, I can clarify with more brevity. Deductive reasoning leads to a valid conclusion when the premise is known to be true therefore the conclusion is true. For example, all men are mortal, and Dave is a man, are premises known to be true. This being the case the conclusion that Dave is mortal also must be true.

In our bin scenario, Dave's premise that all the neighbours had put out yellow bins led him to conclude it was yellow bin day. But he is no Sherlock Holmes, and his reasoning was in fact inductive not deductive. Inductive reasoning uses specific but limited observations to draw a general conclusion that can be applied more widely. In this case all, or at least the majority, of the bins Dave could see were yellow and he based this conclusion on a premise which had only limited observations and therefore not known to be universally true. Once I walked up to the brow of the small hill, I could see that all the residents beyond the brow had put out green bins.

Unimpressed by my revelation, Dave dismissed the residents on the eastern side of the street and went with his western side peers. I suspect there was a degree of snobbery here where he regarded his more immediate neighbours as more erudite. I, on the other hand can best be described in this instance as a sheep, so I followed the leader and we both put out the yellow bins. Had we hit the nail firmly on the head? Or was it lambs to the slaughter? Education is a marvellous thing and at least I can see inductive reasoning when it hits me in the face.

DAY TWO HUNDRED AND FIFTY-FIVE

The bin men came and collected the green bins.

Bastards.

DAY TWO HUNDRED AND SIXTY-FOUR

The next few entries in the diary may occasionally have a more exotic feel as I am traveling with the love of my life to foreign climes. Namely South Korea and Japan. Now fear not, I realise I am no great travel writer so you will not be getting a budget version of Jack Kerouac, Earnest Hemmingway, or Bill Bryson. Just a few astute or not so astute observations.

In travel and life generally, Kerryn regards my approach as, at best, random and at worst cluelessly incompetent. The list is too long to record here, but examples include my apparently archaic ideal of always wanting to carry cash and a physical credit card as opposed to one held electronically on the mobile. My apparently irrational fear, borne from senility, that situations will arise where only cash is accepted is a constant source of irritation to her. My fear on the electronic card scenario is that if one loses or breaks one's phone then one's life is totally buggered in this online world we live in. Apparently, she packs suitcases better than me and never forgets anything. The list of travel related criticisms (the main ones) laid on me just prior to departure to the airport were:

- ❖ My packing was crap I will have forgotten something in the untidy morass,
- ❖ Everywhere will accept credit cards on her phone so why bring cash,
- ❖ My single plug adaptors are rubbish, best to take large bulky all-purpose universal ones,
- ❖ I am slow getting through the airport and there is always a problem with me and my passport.

Well at the airport there were early signs that the senile old fool was going to come up trumps for this trip. Scrabbling through her handbag at the airport she swore out loud to the horror of those nearby. I just shrugged and looked apologetic of her behalf. She had forgotten her sunglasses and hat. I hadn't.

Travel score: Kerryn 0 Senile old fool 1.

Arriving at the other end in South Korea, Kerryn found herself stuck with the immigration official as the electronic declaration forms would not scan (I suggested on the plane that we fill in the manual forms given to us by the air crew but was overruled). She trotted off to fill in a manual form and returned to the immigration official whilst I did mine. Consternation from an angry security guard drew my attention to a potential bomb threat until I managed to retrieve her hand luggage which she had left unattended at the table where she had filled in the manual form. Unusually flustered, the erstwhile perfect traveller marched past the official once her passport was stamped. I, on the other hand, sailed through serenely without incidence once I had convinced the guard that her handbag did not contain an explosive device. That was two further wins for the old fool, manual declaration forms required and Miss perfect leaving her bag unattended.

Travel score: Kerryn 0 Senile old fool 3

Her woes had not ended as our cab pulled up to the hotel and she tried to pay the fare but her electronic credit card was not readable to the driver's handheld device. She marched off to the reception desk whilst I paid with my physical credit card and dragged our suitcases some yards behind. After form filling the hotel receptionist asked for a card to hold a deposit. Once again, her electronic card did not work so she scrambled in her handbag for her own physical card only to discover that she had apparently picked up the wrong pile when packing and whilst she had her gym card and Australian medical card which were of no use in South Korea, she had not taken her physical credit card. Once more I stepped up to save the day placing my physical card into the receptionists' handheld device and it worked. That's physical card needed to pay the taxi, her failure to pack her own physical card and physical card needed to pay the hotel.

Travel score: Kerryn 0 Senile old fool 6

Once we dumped the bags in our room, we decided to venture out and headed straight for the nearest subway station. Kerryn decided to leave her Ipad to charge whilst we were out and pulled out her bulky universal adaptor which was too big and unwieldy to fit into the narrow space where the socket was situated. I once more saved the day using one of my smaller adaptors specific to the country. I, of course, made no comment. This had become a rout.

Travel score: Kerryn 0 Senile old fool 7

Despite the winter season, the sun shone brightly, and I put on my sunglasses. Kerryn hunted for hers and you may recall (although she didn't in that moment) that she had forgotten to pack them. Once inside the subway system we set about trying to purchase tickets. Having spent ten minutes at the vending machine failing to make her electronic credit card work, I then stepped in with my wad of South Korean Won and fed notes into the required slot. Coins tinkled in a small metal well as my change was dispensed and the machine spewed out two tickets. Apparently in the modern digital world that Kerryn uses as a stick to beat my luddite ways, the machines here would only take cash. Cash, as the old time saying goes, is King.

Which whilst a dated concept with its appallingly gender biased language, it still held true for the Seoul subway system.

Travel score: Kerryn 0 Senile old fool 7

For one of us, it had been a long day.

DAY TWO HUNDRED AND SIXTY-SEVEN

Whilst we had dismissed the idea in the holiday planning stages, we decided that before we leave Seoul, we would visit the Demilitarised Zone (DMZ) which is a two and a half mile wide and one hundred- and sixty-mile-long buffer zone between North and South Korea. This zone was created following the Korean war in the 1950's. It was established under a joint agreement between North Korea, China, and the United Nations. I won't bore you with the history, but I have to say it is an interesting place and well worth a visit. As it turned out it is now also a place on my long list of unusual parts of the earth where I have met Leeds United supporters. My list is extensive and ranges from a queue to a NBL basketball game in Madison Square Garden to Bali. Elsewhere in the world from a small town in Brazil, a Norwegian fjord, and a Kenyan Wildlife Park. This location however probably makes the number one.

In many ways the DMZ reflects the differences in thinking between the North and the South. The North play all sorts of propaganda over loudspeakers whilst the South Koreans play K-Pop all day which is a music trend that is taking over the world – not my world I can tell you. It transpired from my learnings that despite the signed agreement by those pesky China backed North Koreans, they were way too sneaky. Over time, the South Koreans discovered several tunnels under the zone constructed by their cunning neighbours for a future military invasion. It just goes to show that you can't trust anybody nowadays. Again, as a demonstration between the cultural divide, what is an invasion tool for the North is a tourist destination for the South.

Having descended a hundred metre slope to find myself eighty metres underground, I then walked a further two hundred metres under the DMZ At the end of this trek I met three other tourists who were speaking English and noticed that their accents sounded northern (and more accurately, the twang was Yorkshire. They eyed my beanie, which discreetly had the Leeds United logo on it, and we became instant friends. Eighty metres underground and hundreds of metres along a tunnel under the Korean demilitarised zone I met three Leeds United supporters. It became number one on my 'most unusual places to find a Leeds fan' list.

DAY TWO HUNDRED AND SEVENTY

Left Seoul today and headed for Japan. Osaka to be exact. Checking out of the hotel life handed one final ignominy for Kerryn, who's usual razor-sharp efficiency had been called into question. At breakfast, a staff member had sidled up to me to explain a terrible mistake they had made. He showed me the credit card payment that Kerryn had authorised, and it appears they had inadvertently keyed an extra zero on the amount of money owing, which consequently turned our $1,100 dollar bill into $11,000 and to make matters worse Kerryn signed it off at the time. Now if I had overpaid a bill by $10,000, I shudder to think how the conversation would have flowed. I kept calm, in fact I kept quiet, and the money would be refunded or so we hoped. We were told it may take three days. Surely an overpayment of $10,000 dollars is worth a hat-trick.

Travel score: Kerryn 0 Senile old fool 10

DAY TWO HUNDRED AND SEVENTY-TWO

We are in Japan. Generally, I found the Koreans to be very different to the Japanese save for one noticeable habit. I don't know whether the issue is cultural or generational, but the older people were as guilty as the younger ones. So, I am settling on cultural.

Eating in the Executive lounge (get me, Executive lounge – Kerryn is an Accor member), food would be placed out each evening, buffet style, for the hordes of guests who were granted access to descend and devour. Whereas Kerryn and I, with appropriate Western reserve, would take a small plate and put on one or two items and return for more if desired, the Japanese and Koreans had no such reticence. Each would have a minimum of five plates piled up so high that there was an even money chance that it would topple before they reached their tables. Plates never did topple because this lot were seasoned experts. It was hard to get our heads around this behaviour. They were in the lounge, so they clearly weren't short of a bob or two and presumably not been starved for several days. The plates would often have an eclectic mix of food stuffs with little regard for the demarcation of sweet, savoury, entrée, main course, or dessert. A small skewer of beef could be accompanied by a jar of panna cotta, a bread roll, and a piece of sashimi. Once the statutory five plates had been gathered, piled so high that they almost obscured their friend sat across the table, they would then take out their phones. Hundreds of pictures of the piled plates would be taken, then posted to friends and family by which time the erstwhile hot food must have been cold. Why do people photograph food?

Seeing a Korean woman who was barely 50kg devour a volume of food that was half her body weight in one sitting was a thing to behold.

DAY TWO HUNDRED AND SEVENTY-SIX

After several days of stressing, Kerryn confirmed her ten-thousand-dollar error had been refunded.

Rather than bore you with high finance I thought it was worthwhile focussing on health and hygiene matters. For whatever reason, my normally regular toilet visits had ended abruptly. Whilst Kerryn is more used to this scenario, I had a greater level of anxiety because in day-to-day life at home I was as regular as a police speed trap. So off I trotted to the local chemist, which in Osaka was surprisingly hard to find. Maybe people are generally healthier than in Australia.

Eventually I found a small boutique chemist shop with a young woman and a man of a similar vintage to me both wearing white coats. She came from behind the counter to help, but her English was only slightly better than my Japanese and the word 'constipation' was way beyond her limited vocabulary. Naturally, I resorted to international sign language by demurely simulating the act as best I could so as not to cause offence. My acting was obviously Oscar worthy, because my acting hit the mark quickly and she handed me a packet of what I assumed were laxatives. However, it was a case of 'well done but no cigar,' I was pretty sure that these were not suppositories and looked more like a packet of tablets. Free medical advice from yours truly; oral laxatives never work.

There followed a short physical mime session which would have done Marcel Marceau proud, where an old western man, me, gesticulated his needs to a young Asian woman. I vigorously pointed to my mouth and shook my head, then to my arse and nodded encouragingly. If a police officer had entered the shop at that moment, I would have been arrested for attempting to solicit sexual favours. At this point, the older pharmacist came round, ushered his assistant back behind the counter and stood facing me. All that entered my mind was a scene from 'Way of the Dragon' where Bruce Lee (in this case the old Osakan pharmacist) faced up to a Chuck Norris (in this case me). And I can tell you that from memory Chuck Norris came off worst. He, the pharmacist not Bruce Lee, then went into a strange crouch, and I was waiting for Bruce's signature high pitched squeal before he launched himself at me.

My fears were, of course, unfounded. From his bent position he reached back with his right arm, extended his index finger, and started a machine-like prodding action towards his own posterior. It all clicked. I nodded and he picked another packet from the shelf below, smiled, gave one final prod of his behind and then shook the packet to confirm that this was what I wanted. I didn't know what to do and, in my relief, I bowed (it was in Japan after all) and he reciprocated with his own bow.

DAY TWO HUNDRED AND SEVENTY-SEVEN

A substantial portion of this day was spent on the toilet.

One of the best things about Japan, and South Korea for that matter, is the humble toilet, which in these countries is far from humble. If you've ever been on one, you'll know what I am talking about. Technologically, they are works of digital and engineering genius. Admittedly as all the buttons are labelled in Japanese (or Korean) they take a bit of time to master but, in my opinion, they are the best invention since the wheel. Even after a particularly strenuous and challenging session, as I had post suppository, you rise from that wonder of modern appliances far cleaner than when you started. There are more features available than you would have thought possible for a device that accommodates such a basic human function. I am particularly impressed by the laser accuracy of the cleansing water jet which gives you a pleasant tingle in the most unexpected of places.

I am interested in purchasing one, but uncertain whether any Australian plumber would be capable of repairing it in case of a malfunction. You would need an electronic engineering degree.

DAY TWO HUNDRED AND EIGHTY-TWO

I am back in Australia so no more insightful observations about foreign cultures. If you want those, I recommend your read, the aforementioned, Jack Kerouac, Earnest Hemmingway, or Bill Bryson.

We've been invited to a wedding later in the year. The lamb to the slaughter is Kerryn's cousin, Simon, who lives in Sydney. Jokingly I said to Kerryn I guess we are going to have to fork out for flights and hotels again. When Simon's brother got married, he chose Daydream Island for the event which was a long haul over to the east coast then onward to an island. It wasn't cheap. Before I could trot out my usual suggestion that perhaps they could get married in Perth for once, Kerryn cut me off saying "actually they are not get married in Sydney." She went on to explain that it will be held at his partner's hometown which happens to be Cordoba. That's Cordoba, Argentina.

Kerryn got straight onto the arrangements whilst I contemplated a visit to the bank to get out a second mortgage.

DAY TWO HUNDRED AND EIGHTY-EIGHT

Humour is a funny old thing. Sometimes I think I'm from another planet or my delivery is too deadpan for the Australian palate. I attempt several quips during the day but tend to get limited responses if the humour is too dry. American humour is devoid of irony, so I am used to this when talking to them and Australian humour at its best is self-deprecating and hits you in the face. English dry humour, to the non-English, is an acquired taste. Two examples today which demonstrate my point.

During the morning, the doorbell rang and Alfie leapt into home defence action. I only just managed to get to the door without breaking my neck he rushed past me barking furiously. The Postie, not Mister Mutunga who had moved on to greater things in the Australia Post hierarchy, stood holding a parcel. Being of Caucasian origin the new Postie presented less of a threat in Alfie's eyes, and he retreated behind my legs (Alfie, not the Postie).

Waving the parcel the Postie said to me, "Sorry to disturb you but this parcel is for next door."

My response was, “well, in that case you’ve delivered it to the wrong house.”

I could see he did not know how to respond. Returning his perplexed stare with a smile I decided to put him out of his misery and assure him that, as usual, I would give it to them when they returned home.

Example two came during a conversation with Brenton, who is Simon’s brother. We were talking about the Argentinian wedding. Brenton has a young son, Danny, who is about to start school. Brenton told me he was trying to teach Danny a couple of Spanish words to impress the locals at the wedding but was having no luck. Danny wasn’t getting it.

“I can’t even get him to say ‘Please’ in Spanish,” he moaned.

My response was “that’s poor for four,”

Not even a glimmer.

DAY TWO HUNDRED AND NINETY

Got a text from teenage son.

English as a language is a dying art.

Complete words are rarely used during texting which, let's face it, is the primary source of conversation nowadays. Younger people question why I would call them to talk when I could have texted. This is all very well if you know the language, but I can easily get a text which is incomprehensible to me.

All I can say is "OMG, WTF, TBH I'm SMH, AFAIK FWIW it's all incomprehensible. If you do understand it, PLMK.

DAY TWO HUNDRED AND NINETY-FOUR

Switched on the radio today and up popped that pop classic by Bucks Fizz, "Making your mind up." Older readers will recall the video where halfway through the song the two male singers rip off the women's longer dresses to reveal miniskirts. Setting aside all sorts of political correctness issues I did think elements of the song lyrics were 'questionable' especially given the sexualised images in the video. For example, "don't let your indecision take you from behind." This line of thought then led me down the reminiscence path of a whole load of songs in my childhood days which would be cancelled now if any of the thought police got hold of them. But at the time people of all ages just sang along with naïve innocence.

Where to start. There is a great sixties hit, 'Young Girl' by Gary Puckett and the Union Gap which is about a bloke who chases a girl under the age of consent then looks for plaudits because he managed to keep his old fella firmly in his pants. For the period this was a case of art not mimicking reality as history has taught us about many others in the music industry, especially disc jockeys, who didn't follow the example of the bloke in the song.

A massive worldwide hit in the 70's was 'In the Summertime' by Mungo Gerry. In the song our Mungo cheerfully sings "have a drink, have a drive," after which you should "speed along the lane, do a ton or a ton and twenty-five." The Government picked up on this and used the song in a drink driving campaign with a very eerie ending. This little ditty also encouraged a rather disrespectful approach to dating. "If her daddy's rich take her out for a meal, if her daddy's poor just do what you feel."

And finally, though there are thousands more, the dear old Beatles and a song from their iconic Sgt Pepper's album, 'Getting Better.' We are talking domestic abuse here. "I used to be cruel to my woman; I beat her and kept her apart from the things that she loved."

The great irony of this era is that all the above, and much, much more, flew under the radar whilst an inoffensive song, sung tongue in cheek by a black American singer, caused a ruckus and was banned from being played on many UK radio stations. Mister Chuck berry, nicknamed the Father of Rock and Roll, released a song called "My Ding-a-Ling." The ding-a-ling referred to in the song is a toy consisting of silver bells hanging on a string. Now doubtless he sang it with a wry smile and doubtless you could substitute "ding-a-ling" for "penis" and the song would still make sense … even if it didn't scan. But seriously, compared to the other stuff mentioned above what's the problem. I think the uptight morality campaigner, Mary Whitehouse, couldn't see the wood for the trees (if you'll forgive my old school innuendo).

DAY TWO HUNDRED AND NINETY-SIX

Whilst out taking Alfie for a walk in the local park I came across a sign that definitively demonstrates the ability of bureaucracies to miss the point. It was a newly erected sign that gave the unequivocal command that no golf balls are allowed. Whether or not you feel this is reasonable, it certainly doesn't pass the consistency and common-sense test. I can cast your mind back to day forty of this diary when I had an encounter with a discus chucking gorilla. When I raised that issue with the council I was greeted with the administrative equivalent of a shrug. They decided no action was to be taken and certainly no signs required in this instance. It is clearly alright to launch a two-kilogram aerodynamic weight at speeds of almost sixty miles an hour into an area frequented by infants and pensioners. Conversely the council feel it is not acceptable to take a forty-five-gram golf ball onto the park even if all you wanted to do is a spot of putting practice. Go figure.

I carried on with my walk pondering this mystery when my attention was drawn to a young girl with a poodle on a lead. She was stood watching her dog engage in what we euphemistically called 'a number two.' A few yards ahead of her a man was waiting and when the dog had finished, she dragged it off to join him. They proceeded to walk on. Of course, I could not let this go being one of those people who, in childhood, perpetually had canine faeces on the sole of my shoe. I caught up to him and asked the obvious question, "did you realise your dog had done a shit mate?"

Adopting an expression of surprise, he replied, "Oh! What? Really?" I suspect that the acting in his ten-year-old daughter's school play would be of a higher standard than his performance, but I played along assuming he was just trying to save face. He made a big show of asking his daughter if Fido had indeed performed the alleged act and she, to her credit, admitted that he had. At that point I assumed that it was job done, and my attention was diverted to Alfie who, with all the poo talk, decided to indulge himself and was rapidly spinning in preparation of the act. By the time Alfie had finished spinning (refer day one hundred and seventy-two) and then pooing, the father and daughter were two hundred metres away scuttling towards their car. It was, I reflected as I transferred Alfie's effort into a custom designed bag, what the Australians colloquially call, a dog move.

DAY TWO HUNDRED AND NINETY-NINE

Received a letter from our gas provider today. It started in quite a cheery way explaining that they had been unable to access my property to read the gas meter and as a result had to estimate the last three bills. Three paragraphs in, the tone changed to 'enough is enough, estimates won't cut it anymore' and became more officious. The letter explained that my contract with them required me to provide safe and unrestricted access to my property to enable them to read the meter. This was followed by a short one-line paragraph baldly stating that, 'It's a safety issue, too.'

They proceeded to follow this ominous warning with a lecture explaining that it's not just about accurate billing. It's a safety issue because, without access, they are unable to perform the maintenance that keeps the meter in safe working order. Can't say I've ever seen a meter reader doing any maintenance.

The letter then reverted to its original cheerful inclusive vibe with the suggestion that we work as a team. Like old mates they asked me to give them a call to arrange for the meter to be read.

Harking back to my brief cub scout career (that's another story which I won't bore you with), I remembered that one can never be too prepared. Prior to making my call I popped outside to read the meter so that I would be armed with all the pertinent information. Indeed, I believed it would be more efficient for all concerned to give them the actual reading. I had become caught up in the spirit of their call to arms at the end of the letter, which was, quote, 'Let's work together to fix this."

Thirty-five minutes later I was growing tired of listening to 'call holding' music interspersed with robotic assurances that I had moved up the queue and my call would be answered shortly. My team spirit had become jaded and when I was finally greeted with a human voice rather than a robot's, I admit to being a little irritable. What then followed was a further twenty questions from the call centre person who finally paused for breath after obtaining my account number, surname, address, partner's name etc. This momentary lull in the interrogation afforded me the opportunity to explain the purpose of my call. But I wasn't quick enough and despite getting out half a sentence she talked over me. As the Germans say in dated old war films, "Ve vill ask the questions."

It transpired that I still had to prove that I was who I was claiming I was. If you get my drift. Thus followed a further battery of questions such as full (including middle) name, date of birth, blood group, height, weight, sexual proclivity, and email address. At this point forty-five minutes had passed since I dialled 13 13 58. In an exasperated attempt to end the interrogation I begged for the opportunity to explain the purpose of my call to which she replied that it was vitally important that my identity was fully verified.

There was more security involved in arranging a meter reading than entering Fort Knox. With half-hearted sarcasm (I was mentally shot) I asked why anybody would fraudulently call the gas company with the malicious and evil intent to arrange access to a meter at another person's property. Irony was met with silence. My wish was finally granted when I gave the last piece of information she had requested, namely my mobile number.

I explained the purpose of my call (now fifty minutes since I dialled) and offered a solution. Having read the meter and taken a picture, I helpfully offered to give the reading over the phone and/or send the picture (if the call centre lady would be so kind as to give me an email address). No visit needed, less hassle for the gas company and cost efficient. Surely a win-win situation if ever there was one. I waited expectantly for praise.

An audible sigh came down the phone followed by an explanation that the meter had to be physically seen by one of their operatives. I pointed out that the letter suggested we should work together, and this attitude exuded a distinct lack of trust on the part of the gas company and a serious slur on my integrity.

Another audible sigh, followed by a repetition of the requirement for a physical visit.

Surrendering to the weight of the gas company's bureaucracy I capitulated and agreed a suitable day for the momentous event. I asked what time suited them for the appointment and was offered two slots. It turned out that their idea of a 'slot' was very different from mine. It was more of a gaping sinkhole than a slot. The call centre lady patiently explained that they could offer a visit at some point between 7am and midday or, if that did not suit, midday and 5pm.

Caught between outrage and speechlessness I offered a final but futile act of resistance by pointing out the obvious. Surely a five-hour slot for a thirty second appointment is unreasonable and a total disregard for my, or any other customer's, time. All I could do was splutter a redundant question, "You expect me to hang around five hours for a thirty second appointment?" When receiving the answer 'yes,' I pathetically muttered that in the timeframe offered approximately 600 meters could be read.

Defeated I took the midday to 5pm slot.

Teamwork makes the dream work.

DAY THREE HUNDRED AND ONE

There is a building site behind Dave and Brenda's house which has been an ongoing battle for the past fifteen months. Having demolished the old run-down house, the site has been left as a pile of rubble and sand which, with the south westerly wind, means that every house in the vicinity gets a dust bath every few days. Changing the builder's name for legal reasons, let's call him Dickhead, I have to say that Dave has played an absolute blinder. He has been in contact with Dickhead's office and some poor woman has been the recipient of Dave's angst over the entire period. In her defence she is a bit of a star, an angel with a Dickhead for an employer. She tries her best to address complaints but with a Dickhead for an employer she doesn't have anywhere to go. I won't bore you with the whole story, but the latest drama is that large holes are being dug at the site and, contrary to health and safety regulations, no fencing has been put up.

Phone calls from Dave, Kerryn and myself to every conceivable Government agency and, of course, the ever-pointless Local Authority, have yielded a blank. All bureaucrats typically disinterested despite the fact the danger to local school kids, who inevitably mess around on the site, is brought to their attention.

Dave's commitment can never be doubted, and he is willing to risk life and limb to get a response. When I say risk life and limb, I do not mean his own but those of his grandkids who are left in his charge from time to time. Long story short, we now have furnished the authorities with a photo of unidentified (cough, cough, ahem) infant school children, playing on the site near a big hole.

In any war there is always collateral damage, and one must admire Dave's tenacity in his willingness to sacrifice life for a noble cause. Not his own of course, but his grandchildren.

DAY THREE HUNDRED AND FOUR

It's been a while since I have had cause to converse with local estate agents. It's probably crystal clear by now that I am not the biggest fan of this profession but thanks to my earlier efforts their annoyance factor, in terms of me at least, is quite low. Credit where it is due, they eventually desisted from sending me leaflets about how well they are doing and have remained quiet on the pointless leaflet front. However, I am moved to mention today's effort which I find hard to categorise. I am wavering between, stupidity or simply the laziness of the leaflet delivery person. If I am being generous, I guess I can appreciate that they might be desperate to offload leaflets at any cost to bring this mind-numbing task to a rapid conclusion.

I will allow you to pass judgement on whether this leaflet delivered to me was worthwhile. My conclusion is no but here is what happened.

My mailbox this morning contained a very glossy and professionally produced leaflet with the heading "Just Listed." The photograph is startling familiar as it is the view from my balcony looking directly across the road.

Were you to stand on my balcony you would see that it is impossible to miss the two-metre square sign indicating that the neighbour's house is for sale.

DAY THREE HUNDRED AND EIGHT

Earlier in this diary I have expressed my opinion on those who tout religion and I admit to being perplexed by how seemingly intelligent, educated people hold on to unprovable and contradictory beliefs. I read an article today about a radio show hosted by a woman called Doctor Laura Schlesinger who said that, as an observant Orthodox Jew, homosexuality is an abomination and cannot be condoned under any circumstance. She referenced Leviticus. Now I admit that I have barely a superficial knowledge of religion and much prefer to read more entertaining fiction. Nevertheless, this article spurred me on to look further as this woman clearly was keen to educate pagans like me regarding God's law. Armed with this new knowledge, gifted by Doctor Laura, I can simply inform my gay friends that their life is an abomination because Leviticus says so.

End of debate - let's just have a drink and move on.

But I can't – move on that is.

The problem is that my natural curiosity got the better of me and I read a bit more than the passage referenced by Doctor Schlesinger.

Inevitably the more I read the larger my list of questions grew if I was to follow God's Law as she advised. I could really do with a good three hours in her company to clarify a few points if I am to commit to obeying God's law. It certainly saves a lot of hand wringing about what is right and what is wrong, and I just need to do what I'm told. But first, before I make the commitment, I have a few points to clarify.

1. Leviticus 25:44 says that I may possess slaves providing they are purchased from neighbouring nations. Australia has quite a few neighbours. Does that mean I can own Kiwis and Indonesians or does it also include citizens of Borneo, Papua New Guinea, or Taiwan.

2. Exodus 21.7 sanctions the selling of my daughter. I wonder what Doctor Laura would think is a fair price.

3. I have a neighbour who I caught working on the Sabbath and Exodus 35.2 clearly states he should be put to death. Am I morally bound to kill him, or do I leave this to the local clergy?

4. Whereas I don't burn bulls on the altar as a sacrifice to the Lord who finds the odour pleasing (Leviticus 1:9), I do put the occasional snagger and steak on the barbie. Kerryn however is vegetarian and,

unlike the Lord, does not find the odour pleasing. Should I smite her?

5. Speaking of Kerryn, I realise from Leviticus 15:19 that I am not allowed contact during her time of menstrual uncleanness. I accidently kissed her on the cheek yesterday before I realised my error and I was, according to Leviticus, rendered unclean by this action. So, to rectify my sin, I ran to the bathroom to wash my lips by putting them under the cold water tap which was turned on to its fullest extent. Then I vigorously started to wipe them with her flannel until she took offense and hit me. In this situation am I allowed to smite her back?

DAY THREE HUNDRED AND NINE

I revitalised my attempt at the "auld game" today, which the Scottish originally called 'gouff.' Due to a council funded refurbishment project at the course, it had been a while since I pounded the fairways and greens of the local club. The place looked very different post refurbishment and the old scuzzy bar which was previously exclusively inhabited by the elders of the community, had been wiped off the face of the earth. Gone was the spectre of the Grim Reaper sat patiently in the corner waiting to escort the octogenarians to their final resting place. In its place was an airy, bright new bar with lots of screens showing sports. Mid-morning the place was fully of young mums in their active wear meeting other young mums in their active wear for coffee. Next to them babies were gurgling contently in their push chairs.

What had not changed was the dynamics of the game with my old foes. As usual the scoring was somewhat approximate with scores such at five or six being announced at the conclusion of each hole even though those announcing the scores had clearly played four shots getting out of the woods from a wayward drive. Still, it's not the US Masters.

There was one incident of interest when we went to assist Les who had shanked his drive on the Par Three into a clump of trees. Once the location of the ball was discovered it came with a surprise package. We were presented with the challenge of a six-foot kangaroo stood astride Les's Titleist Pro V1x, with his own balls (the kangaroo's, not Les's) dangling six inches above. Kangaroos, for the uninitiated, tend to have very prominent testes hanging between their hind legs. Five minutes later the stand-off between a slightly pissed off marsupial and three slightly worried retirees ended, and we could resume the game once our friend had hopped off onto the adjoining fairway.

DAY THREE HUNDRED AND THIRTEEN

Today a few of my football teammates attended a funeral of an ex-player. Being a relative newcomer to the club of only two years standing I never knew the bloke, but I think he wasn't much older than me and he died after a long battle with Alzheimer's. Very sad and makes you think about when and how your time will come.

Rather than get maudlin, it left me to ponder on the wisdom I had acquired in old age. Here are some things I can pass on to you, the reader, that I have heard on my journey.

Borrow money from pessimists – they don't expect it back.

A clear conscience is the sign of a bad memory.

Half the people you know are below average.

82.7% of statistics are made up on the spot.

The speed of light is about 300,000 kilometres per second. So, what's the speed of dark?

I'd kill for a Nobel Peace prize.

What's another word for Thesaurus?

If at first you don't succeed, sky diving isn't for you.

And finally … whenever I think of the past it brings back so many memories.

DAY THREE HUNDRED AND FIFTEEN

Bin day tomorrow. Dave and I were, once more, faced with one of the great questions in retired life. Is it the week for the Yellow (recyclable rubbish) bin or the Green (garden organics) bin. From my previous entries regarding this knotty problem, you may remember that these bin debates tend to lead me down the path of various other philosophical questions such as Theseus's ship and the relative merits of inductive logic. This was no different.

Peering down the street Dave announced that, without doubt, it was a yellow bin day, making the bold statement that the thirty plus other people who had put out yellow bins couldn't all be wrong.

Well allow me to disabuse you of the validity of Dave's flawed premise.

The election of the new Pope yesterday sparked my consideration of the bin issue and Dave's bold statement. Two and a half billion people on this earth believe in Christianity. Can two and a half billion people be wrong? If the answer is 'no,' then logically the six billion of the remaining world population who don't believe in Christianity are wrong. Moving away from religion to politics, the orange moron in charge of the United States of America seemed to be claiming some reflected glory in that the new Pope was a native of his country. It was apparently a great honour that the cardinals, via God, had chosen the first north American Pope. Classic narcissism that the election of God's representative on earth was all about him being a yank.

The American debacle was another classic example which counters the 'surely all these people can't be wrong' argument. Seventy-seven million people voted for Trump. Seventy-seven people voted for the first former President to be convicted of a felony to then make him the first convicted felon to be re-elected as President.

Whilst I appear to have digressed from the bin issue, I will bring it back to the issue in hand. Following Dave's logic that thirty plus people can't be wrong, we put out the yellow bins like good earth saving re-cycling citizens.

DAY THREE HUNDRED AND SIXTEEN

The bin men came. It was green bin day.

Bastards.

DAY THREE HUNDRED AND TWENTY-FIVE

Bit of a break since the last entry due to my football tour to Penang. There was a Masters tournament and a Grandmaster's tournament. With the latter being for those sixty years and older, I was looking forward to playing against someone age appropriate for once. It was a seven a side international tournament played on a full-length grass pitch in a constant temperature of thirty-four degrees centigrade coupled with ninety per cent humidity. Being comprised of players from various clubs we were named the Black Swans (the Western Australia State symbol.) Along with two of my Subiaco teammates, I was selected for the Black Swans B team.

What could go wrong?

Quite a lot, actually.

One player sustained an injury in the first minute in the first of our six scheduled games. For him, the tournament was over before it started.

The rules allowed for a couple of players between fifty-five and sixty in the nine-man squad. Now I know and have observed that those blessed with Asian genetics tend to be well preserved compared to the white, overweight, beer swilling, deep- fried food guzzling westerners with translucent skin tones. But (and there is a 'but') some of these fellas, if over sixty, looked like they had spent the last year bathing in the fountain of youth. In addition, I found, as I was scythed to the ground by a player who looked younger than my eldest (thirty-eight-year-old) son, that the refereeing was best described as laissez faire. The whistle remained eerily silent.

In the bar after the first night, the 1980's classic pop anthem, 'One night in Bangkok', drifted from the speakers around the venue. Although we were in Malaysia, not Thailand, I looked around at the clientele. Some of the lyrics carried a certain relevance and the name Penang, with its two syllables, could have easily been substituted for Bangkok into the song. Particularly …

"One night in Bangkok and the world's your oyster

The bars are temples and the pearls ain't free.

You'll find a God in every golden cloister.

And if you're lucky then the God's a She."

It did make me reflect on the night ahead as I spotted our one single unattached lothario in the team, Greavesie, wandering off into the night. Most likely he was on a mission to seek company that is a tad more stimulating than a bunch of tired, fat, pissed and battered old men.

The second and final day of the tournament brought a certain amount of clarity to the nature of the proceedings. To put it into context, the locals do not possess the wealth of the foreign visitors. Not that we are exactly wealthy but everything in life is relative. According to a reliable source the winners and runners up of the tournaments (and associated referees) received prize money. It suddenly all became clear. For the record, the Black Swans B team won only one game and that was against the Black Swans A team. One victory, but a sweet one providing ample scope for banter at the post tournament drinking session.

DAY THREE HUNDRED AND TWENTY-NINE

Walked downstairs this morning to be assaulted by the usual cloud of Jake's aftershave which had been liberally sprayed around the place. I suspect he gets through several litres of the stuff a year. It must be hard being a six foot four adonis because he spends enough time and resources on his wardrobe and grooming to sustain the GDP of a small African country. At a foot shorter, I never troubled the scorer in the adonis stakes and consequently never really challenged the fashionistas in my youth either.

Obviously in my twilight years I have become invisible as is the destiny of most old people and I certainly haven't improved on the grooming and wardrobe front. So, when I went to the local barber, I was an easy target. The three regular 'hair technicians' were all occupied with other customers. One of the clients had barely had any hair at all, so I thought I wouldn't have to wait long. It transpired that cutting the side bits of remaining hair clinging desperately to the scalp of bald men takes just as long as the kid with the thick unruly ginger mop.

After a couple of minutes, a nervous looking youth who had been engaged in sweeping up the fallen locks, sidled up to me and asked me if he could cut my hair. He was honour bound to reveal that he was a trainee. Looking into his sorrowful but expectant eyes I caved immediately and said that it would be no problem. He had hit pay day selecting a man who, even in the throes of his testosterone fuelled youthful sexual peak, spent limited time grooming … let alone devoting effort during the lost cause of his graveyard years.

Eagerly, the trainee went about his business with his buzzer and scissors with enthusiasm. Finishing with a flourish by sweeping the gown off my body whilst brushing away hair that had fallen on my shoulder, he offered 'product' for my remaining locks. I declined. My initial impression was that the result didn't look too bad when he quickly wafted his mirror around my head.

Later in the day, I discovered that I had to do a bit of minor maintenance to tidy up one or two unruly clumps. Twenty-four hours later I asked a question of Kerryn that I had never asked her before. On the other hand, she had asked me this many times. It's a question, if posed by a female to a male, that is as deadly as a spring loaded improvised explosive device.

"What do you think of my hair?"

She took off her glasses and then turned to look at me, which is proof of my permanent invisibility. Imagine if, after twenty-four hours, I had not only failed to comment on her hair but had not enthusiastically eulogised about it. Her reply was "It looks okay, a bit long."

If the apprentice has heard this assessment, he'd be on cloud nine. (Irony alert).

DAY THREE HUNDRED AND THIRTY-ONE

Had the pleasure of the company of the Jehovah witnesses once more today. It had been quite a while, so I was happy to trot on down to our front door for a chat. They were working in pairs as usual, and the spokesperson greeted me with a cheery smile which I duly returned once I had quietened down Alfie. As well as racist he is clearly agnostic if not antagonistic towards the Christians.

"I would like to bring you good news today," announced the spokesperson.

At this point a whole sackful of hopeful thoughts crossed my mind. Leeds had already been promoted to the Premier League, so I was sure it was not football related. Someone had successfully assassinated Trump, or I had won the Jehovah lottery. The sack of hope burst and emptied when she told me that the good news was something she wanted to read from a scripture, and would I mind if she did this.

"Hang on," I replied. "If you are reading it from the scripture, isn't that over two thousand years old? It can't exactly be classed as news, can it?"

She ignored my question and went ahead with her reading. I zoned out and Alfie gave the occasional impatient woof. I zoned back in when she stopped reading and asked me if I had any questions. I told her one sprang to mind having seen Putin on the news. If God created humankind and God is good how come some of the humans that he/she created are evil?

She gave me a patronising smile as I had clearly missed the obvious answer. Didn't entirely follow her argument, but she talked about free-will and argued that God did not cause evil but allowed it to exist to respect human autonomy. God is a bit of an enigma. On the one hand he is a dictator dishing out commandments and the like, on the other hand he respects the right of self-determination.

My own immediate feeling was that the freedom to be evil is a high price to pay for the millions who have suffered at the evil of a few. In Ukraine we have a Russian dictator who is clearly evil invading a peaceful country and slaughtering thousands each month. God may have given Putin the go ahead to practice pure evil, if it is his (free) will, but those being slaughtered did not have any choice in the matter. So where was their free will?

I suggested that the free will argument may have a few flaws. If Christians believe God is all powerful and all good, there shouldn't be any evil in the world because God wouldn't allow it. Yet evil exists. Either God isn't all powerful (or else he/she would stop evil) or God isn't all good (because he/she has the power to stop evil and chooses not to).

Apparently, the answer is that it is God's divine will and God's reason for allowing evil and suffering is beyond human understanding. Well, I had to concede defeat because it is certainly beyond mine.

Well, there was no way I was going to let them get off that easily. With enthusiasm I announced that I had some news of my own and it was a lot more current than the Bible.

They eyed me suspiciously. Having seen a science program on cosmology the previous evening, I told them about the latest technological development in photography where the scientist on the show displayed an image of a small, by small I mean infinitesimal, portion of the universe beyond our milky way. Each of the bright lights which looked like stars in this minute portion of the universe was, in fact, a whole galaxy each with thousands of stars. The mind-bending vastness demonstrated how very insignificant (gross understatement) earth was in the scheme of things. All the rest, to our knowledge, was uninhabited by life so where does this leave God? Has he/she merely devoted his/her efforts in an extremely small, infinitesimal portion of existence. Isn't this idea at odds with the concept of an omnipotent, omniscient, and omnipresent entity?

I did not have to wait long for a response. They thanked me for my time and left just as I was getting warmed up.

DAY THREE HUNDRED AND THIRTY-THREE

I read the news today, oh boy! (to quote the Beatles).

Day by day it becomes all too clear to any right-thinking sane individual, that Trump is either senile, insane or both. Having gleefully shared images of himself dressed as the Pope saying he didn't create the image but here it is, he is clearly in love with the idea of being God's representative on earth. Setting this aside it seems, in a press conference talking about tariffs, he believes that if he didn't create the earth, he certainly invented the English language. He announced to the world that "basically what we are doing is equalising. It's a new word that I came up with which I think is probably the best word."

So now the insane orange clown thinks he is inventing words that already exist.

I think a better word is "plagiarise," but there are many other words far more appropriate to him. Larceny, corruption, malfeasance, and venality to name a few.

His latest venture is to accept a personal gift of a $400m luxury aircraft from Qatar which given the circumstances and history is frankly astounding. In contrast to gifts from foreign countries to his predecessors, which were donated to the State, he plans to keep the aircraft when he leaves office for his personal use. A President now beholden to a regime that pumped over a billion dollars into Hamas and funded the al-Qaeda supporting emirs of the Taliban. There are many more examples, but you get the picture. In short, he should accept the gift for many reasons, not least because it contravenes Article 1, Section 9, Clause 8 of his country's much-loved Constitution.

That's why you don't put a convicted felon in the White House.

Bertrand Russell summed up the situation quite nicely.

"Many of the actions by which men become rich are far more harmful to the community than the obscure crimes of poor men, yet they go unpunished because they do not interfere with the existing order."

DAY THREE HUNDRED AND THIRTY-NINE

Humour. It's a funny old game. (See what I did there.)

Whilst enjoying a beer after a football training session with a teammate, he recounted his comedy club experience a few days earlier. He went with his wife and another couple who are Jewish. During the act, the comedian made a few Jewish themed jokes which caused the couple to express loudly that they were offended. They marched out of the auditorium. My teammate and his wife were left between a rock and a hard place and followed the couple out. He asked my viewpoint on the matter. So, this is what I told him.

A well-known comedian has a very strong line on those who make the statement, "I am offended." His view is that people who make this statement think it gives them certain rights, but this is wrong. It is nothing more than moaning and has no meaning or purpose therefore should not be respected as a phrase. When people say, "I'm offended by that," his reply is "so fucking what?"

Another famous comedian takes it a step further and suggests that people without a sense of humour should not be allowed to decide what people with a sense of humour are allowed to laugh at. It would be like allowing colour blind people to decide which colours should be on a colour chart.

Having mulled this over, as well as having my own frustrations and concerns with the political correctness cancel culture, I have arrived at the following conclusions.

1. If you don't like a comedian and the views expressed, then don't go to see them. Most people know what to expect with entertainers from their reputation. Live acts will always go much further than what you see on the telly. If they are edgy on the TV screen, then you can bet your life that they will cross more boundaries than Putin on stage.
2. If you are caught off guard, then feel free to leave. Most likely most of the audience won't share your sensibilities.
3. In most cases the performer does not mean or believe what they say. They are not political activists spewing hate. It is an act which they are performing to elicit a laugh, so it is wrong to cancel them. If you don't like them and have not paid to see them then you have already voted with your wallet.

All that said when my mate told me the joke that offended his friends all I can say is that it simply wasn't that funny.

But was I offended? No, see above.

To prove it I'll finish this entry with a joke …

A black, Jewish lesbian walks into a bar with a Catholic Priest ………

DAY THREE HUNDRED AND FORTY-THREE

It is day four of both Dave and I observing (from our respective balconies) our neighbour, (mad) Stan, strolling up and down West Coast highway pushing a wheelbarrow. In all, we calculated that he must have completed thirty return trips and Dave's curiosity finally got the better of him. Biting the proverbial bullet, he went round to Stan's place to investigate. Finding that Stan had created a neat pile of two hundred bricks on his front driveway, Dave took the unprecedented risk of engaging in a conversation with Stan which inevitably ended up being a long and unfulfilling process. This time it was no different.

From what Dave could determine from Stan's rambling narrative, another kind neighbour in the throes of a demolition project had kindly acceded to Stan's request for the unused old bricks. From the kind neighbour's perspective, I guess it made sense. If someone wanted to remove the bricks it saved him a job. The question that Dave posed was the obvious one. Why did Stan want them?

A casual observer of Stans property would assume that the bricks could be put to good use to reconstruct various parts of the dilapidated house.

There were probably more bricks in his newly created pile than currently comprising the walls of his house.

It transpired that this was not the case and Stan's plans remained a mystery, even to Stan.

Dave returned to report that the future of the bricks was uncertain, but Stan was very happy with his haul. Whilst you can question Stan's logic, you can't fault his work ethic and diligence.

DAY THREE HUNDRED AND FORTY-FOUR

Cleaning our balcony this morning led me to my thought of the day.

In contrast to the rest of the animal kingdom, including humans, why is bird shit white?

DAY THREE HUNDRED AND FORTY-FOUR

As I went about my retirement jobs today, I reflected on my daily function compared to Kerryn who still occupies the corporate world. Listening to Kerryn battering away on her keyboard in the study in between highly important sounding phone calls with words like 'Board meeting,' 'SGM,' 'Merger' and 'Strategy,' I am no longer an executive, but I am a 'putterer." Judging by the discussions that Dave and I have in between errant golf shots, we are both experts in the under-rated art of 'puttering.'

'Puttering,' if I stretch the dictionary definition, is something in between pottering and duties. Like many other men in my position, I engage in the act of doing dozens of little chores that no-one knows needs doing, that no-one wants to do and no-one notices have been done. It's the lot of the (usually male) retiree. This hidden task list sits to the side of the task list provided by the partner, in this case Kerryn and in Dave's case, Brenda.

DAY THREE HUNDRED AND FORTY-EIGHT

Found myself in a café today which turned out to be a monumental error of judgement. To say the food was poor is a gross understatement, and I don't think it is likely to be a realistic challenger for an entry into the Michelin Guide. I have previously recounted the unsatisfactory service culture in Perth and the staff in this place would certainly rank highly if there was a Perth Michelin Guide for staff with a shit attitude.

You may have noticed that I just used the word 'shit,' and this word featured heavily in my interaction with the restaurant manager. Having waited an eternity to get our food once ordered, it was clear that whoever put the food onto the plate had spent very little time in the kitchen. A toddler in a pre-school domestic science lesson could have served up better food which was not only clearly undercooked but was stone cold. Presumably, the waiter had decided to leave it on the counter for ten minutes before bringing it to our table. It took little time to decide that the food should be sent back and by this point we had lost our appetite. I miraculously caught the attention of a sullen gum chewing teenager who seemed to have somehow attained the title of waiter and informed him that we were going.

"What about all the food you ordered? It is being cooked now and will go to waste." It took all my will to avoid responding in the appropriate manner – I'm not one to bully children – so I suggested he get the manager. An older man arrived wearing the expression of a bulldog that had just chewed a wasp and asked if there was a problem. I listed out the problems which took a while because he intermittently interrupted me to indicate that I was mistaken. Clearly, he had not seen the food put in front of us, some of which we hadn't even ordered nor tested its temperature. The inference growing with each rebuttal was that we were liars who had no idea what good food looked or tasted like. To end the cycle, I resorted to the that four-letter word explaining that the food, service, attitude, and general ambience of the establishment was 'shit.'

Puffing up his chest, the manager had now gained an elevated position on the moral high ground and berated me for using crude and offensive language.

My gander was up, and it was now my turn to deliver a rebuttal.

I responded with, "The word 'shit' is far from crude and offensive. It is quite a sophisticated and agile word and very appropriate to these circumstances."

“Sorry?” he replied.

I elucidated. “It is a very flexible word. For example, you can add the name of many different animals to the front of that word and get a very accurate description of this establishment and the attitude of those that work within it.”

“Sorry?” he replied.

“Dog, Bull, Horse, Ape, Bat and Chicken. To name but a few.” I then explained.

“The food is like dogshit. Your suggestion to the contrary is bullshit and horseshit. You now are going apeshit, and you must be batshit crazy if you think what you serve is acceptable. You are too chickenshit to admit your mistake and apologise, so it’s time for us to leave.” Jake piped up after we left the café, “dad you missed out Rat.”

No shit.

DAY THREE HUNDRED AND FIFTY-TWO

Nearing the end of my diary I thought, as a parting gift by way of a thank you for reading it, I would give some advice of how to write good (see what I did there).

Always avoid alliteration.

Prepositions are not words to end sentences with.

Avoid cliches like the plague.

Be more or less specific.

Above all else, don't be redundant; don't use more words than necessary; it's highly superfluous. Ask yourself, who needs rhetorical questions?

DAY THREE HUNDRED AND FIFTY-SIX

I received a letter today from one of my all-time favourite group of people – the bureaucrats. You may recall (of course you won't recall, refer day two hundred and twenty-five) my endeavours to get the local council to act rationally in their campaign to insert, what they named in a fit of playful vomit inducing coyness, wombat crossings. I had also backed up Dave's complaint a few weeks later regarding the dust storms created by a local builder which you also won't recall (Day three hundred and one).

In the case of the latter dust storm complaint, the only response I received was to tell me a month later that the case had been closed. No information nor reason proffered; no action taken. I decided to push this matter up the bureaucratic ladder and wrote to the Ombudsman copying the Local Authority's notification of case closure. My query to the bureaucracy police was basic. I simply asked if it was acceptable for a Council to inform rate payers that their case had been closed with no indication of the findings of their investigation (assuming an investigation was even conducted), the conclusions they had drawn and the outcome.

After ten weeks I finally received an answer from the Ombudsman where they did explain the outcome of their own enquiries. Most of their three-page response explained in excruciating detail that I had received a full response to my complaint referenced 00869. This was in fact true, except complaint 00869 related the wombat crossings not the dust storm complaint (Reference 00892) for which I had only been told the case had been closed. They did, to their credit, devote a short passage to the actual subject of my complaint. The opening sentence gave me false hope.

"I understand that the Council informed you by email (Reference number 00892) that the case has now been completed and closed".

At his point I thought I was getting somewhere. They had finally identified the relevant complaint and now I would get an answer. My hope was immediately dashed when I discovered in the second sentence of this short paragraph, that they had circled back to the irrelevant wombat crossing complaint. They suggested "it would be appropriate to continue to engage directly with the Council on this matter."

With a flourish of incompetence, the Ombudsman informed me that they do not propose to take any further action. Clearly, they missed the crucial point that I came to them in the first place because my direct engagement with the Council failed.

I am defeated and, as the correspondence is all by email, I am also robbed of making the grand gesture of tearing up the letter and throwing it in the bin.

Come the revolution …

DAY THREE HUNDRED AND FIFTY-NINE

They say in Yorkshire, "there's nowt so queer as folk." It is a phrase I dismissed as a youngster being the sort of thing that old folk say who were themselves 'queer.' In my dotage I now have a different perspective.

Looking out of our kitchen window I saw Stan busying himself on the building site next to his property. He was crouched down beside two bricklayers who were halfway through constructing a wall which would eventually provide a nice barrier for the owners to avoid having to look at Stan's near derelict house. What Stan was doing was a mystery to me but, whatever it was, it did not seem to bother the builders.

Later in the day the mystery was solved by the ever-reliable Dave. It transpired that in the process of constructing a new pristine wall separating the new owner's property from Stan's dilapidated abode, a small part of the existing boundary wall was shaved off. Despite the new wall replacing the existing pile of loosely formed bricks, Stan decided that the bits of shaved brickwork were his property and went round with his trusty wheelbarrow to collect it. Now he had a small pile of shaved bricks next to his existing pile of bricks culled from the other development across the road (refer day three hundred and forty-three).

DAY THREE HUNDRED AND SIXTY-ONE

Had an interesting little discussion with a couple of Jake's mates who popped in. I was moved to comment that I could not understand half their conversation because they assigned new, and for the record incorrect, meanings to existing words. Examples I quoted were 'drip' which apparently means style and 'slay' (someone who performs well). They were dismissive so I said that they should imagine if wrinklies like me talked to them in old language. They would see how frustrating it could be. Their response was that they could understand our language so what's the problem. Of course, I could not resist taking up the challenge to make my point so I bet them ten dollars I could construct a sentence in old language that they could not understand. If there is one thing to admire about young people, it's their unwavering confidence.

Money placed on the table, and despite several guesses, they lost.

And the sentence?

"I do not wish to discombobulate or accuse each of you of being an ultracrepidarian, but I do not believe I am mumpsimus."

Then, pointing to one of the group who I knew, from their conversation, was currently lovestruck, I added for good measure, "and as for you Nick, are you still in limerence with that callipygous filly?"

My wallet was twenty dollars heavier.

DAY THREE HUNDRED AND SIXTY-TWO

Played golf today. A comedy of errors. The tone was set early before the round. I placed my bag of clubs in the back of Dave's car and two minutes later found him attempting to put his wallet and phone into the pouch of my bag. I discreetly murmured that he was putting his valuables into my bag. Apparently, it was my fault he was putting his valuables in the wrong bag because I had placed the bag in the back of his car – which for the record he told me to do. Dementia looms.

On the first tee Dave took his time to drive off and in the process Nick, Adrian and I tried to supress a chuckle. He thought we were laughing at his expense given his golfing ability, which we weren't. It was the sight of his golf cart taking on a life of its own and slowly trundling down a slope toward the lake. We all did a workable impression of the tune in the Benny Hill show when the old pervert would chase some scantily clad woman with the film speeded up. Giggles turned to guffaws at the sight of Dave dropping his driver and scuttling after the cart to save it from a watery grave.

Collectively it had to be the worse round of the whole group that I had experienced but it was capped off by an errant drive on the last hole from yours truly. The ball flew far and wide but was prevented from going too deep into the trees having bounced off the belly of a particularly large and angry looking kangaroo. Although I could see my ball, I decided that the wise course of action was to take a drop.

DAY THREE HUNDRED AND SIXTY-FIVE

It's the end of the diary and the nearing the end of the grace period for completing my tax return.

Still, the news is good. The taxman/woman was very pleased with my efforts. They wrote to me saying my return was 'outstanding' which is praise indeed as I hadn't even submitted one.

DIARY POST-SCRIPTUM

Some things change; many things don't. Alfie still is slightly racist, but he is learning to hide it. His pre-poo spinning continues to confound.

Local estate agents continue to post glossy leaflets kindly letting me know that they sold a house.

The Local Authority continues to exist, but the reason why remains a mystery.

A week after I finished the diary, Dave and I successfully identified which rubbish bins needed to be put out. For the record it was red and green.

I have not had any more court cases, so my defence record remains one hundred per cent successful.

No-one has improved in my golfing group, but no Kangaroos have been injured in the process.

Erin is singing fly me to the moon.

Mad Stan's pile of bricks continues to grow but no sign of them being used.

The discus throwing hopeful never got selected to represent his country.

I continue to play football, but a much younger team-mate retired after being punched in the face by a scouser. Apparently over 50's football is less gentile than the English Premier League.

I still can't bring myself to believe in the existence of a supreme being, but I guess as retirement progresses, I am getting closer to finding out one way or another.

www.ingramcontent.com/pod-product-compliance
Lightning Source LLC
Chambersburg PA
CBHW010257100726
47904CB00011B/2633

* 9 7 8 0 6 4 5 5 6 3 7 3 3 *